THE
HONOR TRAIL

KUDOS FOR *THE DRIVE*

A NAIL-BITING SENSATION

Set in Texas after the Civil War, two veterans from the opposing sides make for an odd partnership ... Pura and Craig paint a picture of what life was like in the Texas desert as the characters' lives intertwine as they travel on the long cattle drive from Texas to Colorado.

Another surprise involved the two main female characters ... they did not fall into predictable roles [but] Pura and Craig fleshed out their talents and personalities..

Some settlers from the Eastern Seaboard staked claims on land in Oklahoma and literally lived their first winter in holes they dug into the ground. They left their comfortable lives in cities and traded them for lives filled with unending wind, snow, spring storms, maddening loneliness, and near starvation. Wonderfully, Pura and Craig painted many details that allow readers to experience the rural culture and unforgiving locations through which their characters travel.

The book is the first in the Storm Rider series. At the end of the tale the authors leave unanswered questions which makes this reader look forward to the next book in the series.

—Karl Ashley Smith, Five-star Amazon review

THE HONOR TRAIL

Book 2—The Storm Riders Series

PATRICK E. CRAIG
&
MURRAY PURA

A Christian Company
ElkLakePublishingInc.com

COPYRIGHT NOTICE

Cover and Interior Design: Derinda Babcock, Jeff Gifford, Deb Haggerty
Editor(s): Cristel Phelps, Deb Haggerty

PUBLISHED BY: Elk Lake Publishing, Inc., 35 Dogwood Drive, Plymouth, MA 02360, 2024

Library Cataloging Data
Names: Craig, Patrick E. and Pura, Murray (Patrick E. Craig & Murray Pura)
The Honor Trail: Storm Riders—Book 2 / Patrick E. Craig & Murray Pura
200 p. 23cm × 15cm (9in × 6 in.)
ISBN-13: 9798891341616 (paperback) | 9798891341623 (trade paperback) | 9798891341630 (e-book)
Key Words: Westerns; Western fiction books; Western novel; Wester books paperback; women in the West; women outlaws; Western authors
Library of Congress Control Number: 2024932488 Fiction

DEDICATION

The Honor Trail is dedicated to western storytellers Zane Grey, Louis L'Amour, Will Henry, Max Brand, Bill Gulick, and others—writers whose heroes embodied all that is noble and true about the American spirit
—Patrick E. Craig

Dedicated to the memory of cowboy Cecil Orr.
—Murray Pura

ACKNOWLEDGMENTS

When I was very young, Bill Gulick, the author who wrote *Bend of The Snake, The Hallelujah Trail, Roll On Columbia* and many others, was a frequent guest at my Uncle Fred and Aunt Alice Niemi's home in Walla Walla. From Bill, a gentle and hospitable man, I gained a love for writing and especially a love for the beautiful Pacific Northwest.
—Patrick E. Craig

My thanks to Cecil Orr, who taught me about horses and livestock and how to enjoy the freedom of the last true west.

My thanks to the team at Elk Lake Publishing,Inc.— in particular, Cristel Phelps, Derinda Babcock, and Deb Haggerty for bringing *The Honor Trail* to the light of day; to my writing partner, Patrick E. Craig; and to my family and extended family—happy trails!
—Murray Pura

CHAPTER 1

JURISDICTION

He had never been one to dismiss premonitions, no matter how dark they might be. More than once, he had acted on them during the war. They had proven correct and saved his life. Those he'd known to dismiss them had died young at Gettysburg, Petersburg, and scant hours before Appomattox.

Garrett Roads had pulled a good half-hour ahead of his group of riders and pushed his gelding. His insides were gnawing at him. The cattle drive to Denver had taken longer than he'd expected. He'd often worried about the family ranch in Texas, how it was faring, if his sister and her no-good husband had kept things up in these lean years following the War of Northern Aggression. There weren't even Texas Rangers anymore to keep the land safe. Marauders were everywhere, and they didn't just wear Yankee blue.

He knew the lay of the land well. Past a rugged copse of trees, in a few minutes, he'd see the family spread. But smoke stung his nostrils when a stiff October breeze carried it to him. There was the stink of dead cattle and burnt flesh too—after four years of war across pasture lands and farm fields, a smell that would never leave him. He couldn't ignore the frost it put in his blood. Roads nudged Sharpsburg into a fast trot. Something was amiss. He slipped his Remington pistol out of its holster on his left hip and gripped it in his hand. He even cocked it.

It was a Model 1867 Rolling Block that fired a .50 caliber center fire cartridge and would take a mule's head clean off. There was also the Winchester Yellow Boy carbine in its scabbard off his left knee. Roads raised the pistol high over his shoulder. He had not ridden with a cocked pistol since his last cavalry charge in 1865. Lee tried to break through the Union forces surrounding his army and hemming it in. It had not been possible to cut free, no matter how hard Roads's men tried. The Yankees were as thick and feisty as wild boars.

Suddenly, he saw it. The ranch house. It hit him hard. Like a musket ball striking home. It was black and in ruins. Only the stone chimney standing. Smoke still making its way up from the scorched timbers. Broken fences. Bloated cattle on their backs. Two fresh graves. It all rushed into his eyes and mind at once. He held his mount steady and stared. Except for the war years, the ranch had been home all of his life.

It had not been put to torch that long ago. A day. A day and a half at the most. He put Sharpsburg into a gallop.

There was a knot of men there. Seven or eight. Some in Confederate gray. Rifles and muskets lifted as Roads came charging in. He quickly de-cocked his revolver and holstered it. They did not know who he was. He held up both hands after stopping his horse a hundred feet from them.

"I am Garrett Roads," he announced. "I have been driving beef to Denver. This is my family ranch. My sister and her husband were running things. What happened here?"

A round man, a big man, dressed in blue overalls and a buckskin shirt, hauled himself out of the cluster, all the men's firearms remaining on Roads. "Mister Roads, I am Clyde Dewet, the lawdog the Yankees permit to keep the peace in these parts. All I can tell you is neighbors heard gunfire and saw smoke. A rider came to fetch me and my deputies. Some of Terry's Texas Rangers were with me— they been helping me out, and they came along. That was a day ago. Your brother-in-law was still alive. Joby Watkins, wasn't it? And told us what was. The outlaws come for food and drink and some bloody fun—burning, looting, and shooting. Your sister up and pitched in with them, and she being a handsome lady, the gang didn't say no. She shot her husband when he tried to stop her. Joby said their boy got in front of him and took the first bullet. She put the second and third into Joby. We got Doc Stinson out here, and he kept Joby alive for half a day, but he'd lost too much blood."

Roads held up one hand. "Go slow, Marshal Dewet. Marshal, is that correct?"

"Correct, Mister Roads. The Yankee government put me here—" He spat. "—not the people, but I get along with the good folk hereabouts well enough. Listen, sir. I am sorry to have to tell you all this and all at once. It must feel like a load of buckshot."

"I appreciate that, Marshal Dewet. It is indeed a lot to take in." Roads looked at the other men. "I wish to thank you gentlemen for lending a hand here. I am obliged."

The men nodded and lowered their firearms.

"Sorry for your trouble, Granite." One man with scraggly red hair spoke up. "I remember y'all from the war. A man has a right to come home in peace."

Roads nodded. "Thank you, sir. The exploits of the Eighth Texas Cavalry, Terry's Texas Rangers, they are legendary. I remember you fought at Shiloh. Tooth and nail and claw. You stood true at Murfreesboro and Chickamauga as well, I recall. And fought alongside Nathan Bedford Forrest in Kentucky and Tennessee. Gentlemen, we shall have to make a night of it later on. Reluctantly, I must deal with the business at hand."

Roads had used the talking to force his brain to settle. Now he looked at the graves again. "That is my nephew and my brother-in-law, Marshal Dewet?"

"I'm sorry, sir. Yes, sir, Mister Roads."

"And my sister has taken up with the outlaws who burned down our family ranch?"

Marshal Dewet coughed and looked down at his boots for a moment. "There's more."

Roads's head snapped around. "What more?"

"They raided a small town east of here. Witnesses say she killed two lawmen."

"Witnesses say!"

"Broad daylight. Center of town. She was the one who cut them down. And—"

Roads leaned forward in his saddle. "And what?"

"They say she laughed."

"Laughed." Roads repeated the word, trying to grasp what it meant to have his sister with a smoking gun in her hand, laughing over the bodies of her two victims.

"Witnesses say she enjoyed it. That was in the telegram."

Roads stayed in his saddle a few moments longer. Then he climbed down and led Sharpsburg toward the two graves. There were only crude wooden crosses slapped together on both of them. He stopped at the smaller one first. Slowly, he removed his Confederate butternut slouch hat. It had a

4

patch of crossed sabers, its left brim turned up and pinned to the crown with the stars and bars, its ostrich plume, like JEB Stuart's, groomed and shining. Roads had not worn it since the surrender but had kept it packed carefully in a saddlebag. Two days out from the ranch, he had rooted it out and planted it firmly on his head.

"We did not have you a long time, young'un." Roads spoke softly, as was generally his way. "I am not of the opinion everything transpires is meant to be. Or it is willed to be by God. Many things need not have been at all. May you fare better there than you did here. You tried to save your father's life and that must count for something or nothing counts."

Roads moved on to the second and larger grave. "You did not fit my pistol, Joby. It may be your lazy, worthless ways helped spur my sister over the edge of the cliff and onto the rocks. Nevertheless, she made a terrible choice. There was no need to gun you down in cold blood."

He looked up and away. The marshal, his deputies, and Terry's Texas Rangers were staring at him as if there were nothing else to do in all of God's green earth but look at him. Was it his outfit? His new boots, pants, vest, and long riding coat—all black and slick even after the long ride home—the coat and vest tailor made in Denver. Or could they hear him rambling on about his philosophies like some eccentric professor at the Yankee Harvard?

His head had been full on the long trail behind him. Though there'd been company, and pleasant company at that, he'd spent a good number of hours in the saddle apart from the others, riding ahead or lagging behind, trying to puzzle things through. He glanced back at Joby's grave. Now there were more parts to the puzzle that had to be fitted in.

"Not everything that happens, Joby, just because it comes to pass, is good and has its proper place. Many things that occur are not of any value or benefit. But you don't give a hoot. If you sat up and pushed your knot head through the earth, you'd tell me that. If it helps you there in heaven or hell, such wisdom as I may possess did not come from marble halls and ivy towers, but from mud, musket smoke, and men bleeding into the grass. War was my schoolmaster, Joby. War, the gun, and the dead man's hand underfoot. Battle wielded a harsh whip."

Roads donned his slouch hat and led his gelding back to Marshal Dewet and his men. He saw them stare at his throat for a moment and knew they had spotted the scarf that matched the butternut of his cavalry hat. Well, he had never denied he could be a bit of a dandy when it came to looking the part.

"Do you know the gang who burned my ranch, Marshal?" he asked.

"It was the Yancey boys," one trooper spoke up. "From down Six-Shooter Junction ways. Right by the Gulf."

"Not just the Yanceys," another argued. "The Kincaids are riding with 'em too. And the Conners."

"And Ramirez," a trooper added. "And Perez."

"Sounds like an army." Roads looked directly at the marshal. "How many men are we talking about?"

The marshal was chewing. "With your sister, Mister Roads?"

"Colonel will do."

The chewing sped up. "Pardon, sir. Colonel, it is. Eleven, Colonel Roads. Ten men and your sister." He made to spit but stopped himself.

"*Chica bandida,*" one deputy said. He wore a bright red shirt and scarf.

"What's that?" responded Roads.

"I'm sorry, sir."

"Just tell me. An apology is unnecessary."

"Chica bandida. That's what they're calling her. Your sister."

"Who is?"

"Well, everyone is. Right since word got around a woman was riding with The Ten. *Los Diez Hombres.* The gang's just been ten men since '64 and '65. Now ..."

Roads nodded. "Now the Yankee Press has something to sell papers with. Must have been lean years since Appomattox. They'll make a heroine out of her in their typically backward, lopsided way. Well, that can't be stopped. But the gang can be. What about The Ten, Marshal Dewet?"

"Texas law's been after them for years. They'll stay after them."

"But there hasn't been much luck."

"They're slippery as diamondbacks. No, sir."

"The ranch will have to be rebuilt another day. I am duty bound to bring my sister in. I won't have her leaving a trail of dead men behind her from here to Oklahoma."

"That's a tall order, Colonel Roads. You have no jurisdiction."

"It's my sister, sir. That is all the jurisdiction I require. If I must present myself as a bounty hunter, as odious as that may be, I shall announce myself as such. It is a matter of family honor."

The Marshal dug into his pocket. "I don't have any men to spare to help you out. But I can do this." He pulled out the badge for a Deputy US Marshal. "If you all can stomach the US part of it, this will give you all the jurisdiction you need, even outside of the state."

Roads stared at the badge.

DEPUTY US MARSHAL SOUTHERN DISTRICT OF TEXAS.

"Riders coming in!" one trooper shouted.

Roads looked and saw a man and three women approaching the ranch at a brisk trot.

He gently lowered the barrel of the Henry rifle the man closest to him was pointing.

"Practice some Texas hospitality now, gents," he said. "Those riders are my friends."

CHAPTER 2

HONOR BOUND

Carson Budrow rode slowly up to the smoldering remains of the ranch house. Granite stood easily in front of a group of men. Budrow could see his hands—they were far enough away from his guns to take the edge off the men facing him but close enough if things went south, he could shoot the eyes out of at least three before they got him.

Something else caught Budrow's eye. There were two fresh-dug graves with hastily-made markers right in front of the porch. He heard the three horses behind him, but he did not turn. Instead, he kept his hands in sight, but within grabbin' distance of his guns, and looked at the men who were facing Granite. A hard bunch, western men, not a soft face among them.

Nettie Paris spoke first. "What's going on here, Roads?"

Granite nodded at the assembly before him, many of whom held their rifles at ease but usable. "Nettie, this here is Marshal Clyde Dewet and his boys from over at Canadian Crick. We're talking about Alice."

Another woman's voice rang out. "What about Alice, Granite? Is she in one of them graves?"

Granite turned to the voice. "No, Clar-ay, she isn't."

The Marshal shuffled his feet. "Howdy, Captain Black. Didn't know you and Major Paris was riding with anybody since the women rangers busted up."

"We ain't exactly riding with these two-timing buffalo chasers. Just happen to be cutting the same trail."

Budrow felt a flush rise into his face. Brandy looked straight at him when she made her biting remark. Then she looked back at the marshal with a smirk on her face.

"Now what happened to Alice?"

The marshal went over the story again.

"Bull-pucky." Nettie spit on the ground and wiped her lips. "Alice may have shot the no-good skunk, Joby, but I can't believe she shot Jimmy. She loved that boy."

Brandy Claret Black, who Garret affectionately called 'Clar-ay' after her middle name, pushed her horse forward. "I think you boys are in the wrong state. Alice Watkins never done none of what you said."

"We got witnesses, Brandy. The best. Joby himself. The doc kept him alive for part of a day, and he told us the whole story. And after she rode off with Clive Yancey, him and his gang tried robbin' a bank over east. Two deputies tried to stop them. They had Clive in a box, dead-to-rights, and Alice rode right in with pistols blazing and shot them both. Least that's what it says in the telegram."

One last rider joined the group. She was of a different cut from the two Texas gals but just as striking. Her voice, when she spoke, had the soft melodies of the south, and a couple of the boys in confederate gray looked up and smiled.

"Sorry it took me so long. I'm not quite as saddle broken as y'all. What's going on, Kit?"

Budrow looked over at Annette Devereaux. She had changed a lot since Budrow first met her in the barn on her plantation in the last year of the war—a meeting that had found her naked to the waist and holding off three drunken rape-minded Union soldiers with a razor-sharp pitchfork. But Scat Jansen and his brother and cousin were dead, so the past was the past. Except ...

Budrow pushed Ranger next to Sharpsburg, dismounted, and the two men looked at the ruined ranch house and the two hastily dug graves. Budrow put his hand on Granite's shoulder. "This is terrible, Granite. What are you going to do?"

Roads pushed his guns down into their holsters and tied them back down. "First, I'm going to give my kin a decent burial and a decent marker. I don't want them just stuck in the ground, I want them in the family plot over yonder under the cottonwoods. Then I'm gonna have a drink and consider my options."

One man, a Confederate by his ragged pants, spoke up. "I'll help ya, Colonel. I'm a good hand with a carving knife."

Several voices spoke up.

"Me too, Colonel."

"Get some shovels, boys."

Granite nodded his appreciation. He pointed over at the barn, which was still standing. "I thank you for your help, men. Should be some shovels and a couple of planks in the barn."

While the men went to get what they needed, Granite led Sharpsburg into the shade of the giant oak that towered over the packed ground in front of the steps which once led up to the porch. He sat down and leaned against the tree. He pulled a small flask from his vest and took a long pull. Budrow walked toward Roads, but Nettie touched his sleeve.

"Leave him be, Budrow. He's gonna be grieving for a spell."

***

It was dusk. The long rays of the setting sun brushed the hillsides surrounding the small valley holding the old Roads Ranch. The shadows of the trees and fences spread over the pastures close to the house. Gold, red, and pink bands filled the Texas sky with color. To the east, the indigo of night was creeping westward, and one by one the stars were winking on. The setting sun reflected off the small crick running through the green fields and turned it into a band of gold.

Granite Roads stood by the two new graves now inside the white picket fence that held two older graves with simple carved headstones. Granite pulled a cheroot from his pocket. He offered one to Budrow, lit the match on his boot heel, and the two men stood smoking as the twilight gathered.

One headstone read "Johnston Roads, 1800–1862." The second said, "Mary Roads, A Good Wife. 1810–1845." Next to them, the two fresh graves had wooden crosses with just names—"Joby Watkins-Kin," and "Jimmie Watkins-Nephew."

Granit pointed to the two headstones. "My ma and pa. My ma died when me and Alice were kids. Fever carried her off. My pa never quite got over it. Made him mean, I think. That's why me and him never got along. When I left to join the Confederate Army, he gave the ranch to Alice and drank himself to death."

Budrow shook his head. "I guess we all got something that eats at us, Granite. I'll tell you mine someday."

Granite sighed. "Where are the girls?

"They put up in the bunkhouse. I made us a couple of beds in the hay barn."

"Well, Budrow, this is a real hullabaloo. My kin dead, my sister run off with the worst gang of owlhoots east of the Pecos, and us surrounded by three women that would just as soon shoot us as look at us."

"Yeah, our plan didn't work out so well, did it?"

Roads chuckled. "It all sounded so easy around the fire that night, Budrow. Nettie and Clar-ay were nursing gunshot wounds, and Annette was off in Denver with her pa. You didn't have the sand to pick between Nettie or Annette. And I, like a fool, offered to help you get out of your fix."

"Yeah, just ride off into the sunset and leave the girls to stew in their own juices."

"I guess we forgot Brandy Clar-ay is the best tracker in Texas since Kit Carson. And Nettie most likely figured we would head for the Canadian to see Alice. So, three days out, they caught us."

Budrow grinned. "No flies on those girls. What I don't figure is how Annette got back in time to ride with them."

Granite shook his head. "You got nothin' to grin about, Budrow. Your goose is cooked, and you got three of the baddest females in the west ticked at you. I guess ticked is a mild term. If they could consign you to roast in hell in your own blood, they would. And me? I stumbled into your little mess like the simple jackass I am. Shoot fire and go naked."

"Well, we better head over and take our medicine."

***

Nettie Paris stirred the coals in the fireplace with an iron tong. The bunkhouse at the Roads/Watkins Ranch was first class with a kitchen, running water from the crick outside and comfortable bunks. Nettie was angry and confused. Annette came and stood beside her.

"I think we got ourselves a dilemma, Nettie."

"You mean that horse's ass, Budrow?"

"Yep, that's the one."

Nettie turned to Annette. "What did you have to come butt in for? Me and Kit was doing great. You tell me you love him as much as me, and I'll saddle up and ride out of here."

Annette put her arm around Nettie's shoulder. Nettie tried to shrug her off, but Annette held her.

"That's the problem, Nettie. I don't know if I love him. I think it's more like an infatuation coupled with gratitude for what he's done for me. Oh, yeah, I know I got him all stirred up at the dance in Denver, but I think I was just trying to prove I'm as much of a woman as you and Brandy."

Nettie looked at Annette. "You don't have to worry none about that. You've changed a lot since I first met you. Besides being drop-dead beautiful, you've learned to handle a .50 caliber pistol like an old Texican. I'm proud of you, Annette, even though I'm as jealous as a tomcat on a fence."

"Well, Nettie, I wouldn't be any good if y'all hadn't taught me how to be a western woman. I thought I would always be a pale-skinned, pasty-faced mistress of a plantation in the south. But when the war forced me and my father out west, I think I really discovered for the first time who I was meant to be. And I have you and Brandy to thank."

Brandy got up off her bunk and came over to the fire. "From what the boys told me, you didn't just give that showdown with Skin Ricketts a lick and a promise. You stood right up to those coyotes and sent them to their just rewards. Takes a heap of woman to do that."

Annette smiled. "Tell you the truth, I'd rather ride with you girls than Budrow and Roads. Kit has got himself wound in a knot, but I think he really loves you, Nettie. And I'm willing to let you sit in the bow of the boat and keep my oar out of the water."

Nettie looked at Annette. "You telling me honest, girl?"

Annette grinned. "I should smile, I am."

Nettie's eyes narrowed. "Say, girls, whaddaya say we put a job up on those sidewinders. They snuck outta town like the coyotes they are. Thinking they could get down to Texas and leave us up in Colorado cooling our heels. They had a lot of nerve trying that."

Annette's eyes got a mischievous glint. "What do you want to do to them?"

"I think we should play them as cold as ice. But I also think we should stick to them like white on an egg. These boys need to suffer. They ain't goin' nowhere without us."

Brandy nodded. "I'm in. That Granite needs a lesson. I know he's going after Alice. It's a matter of honor for him. But I think there is more to the story than meets the eye. I've known Alice since we was kids. I just can't believe things happened the way the marshal said. So I need to be there when the showdown comes."

Just then, there was a knock on the door.

Brandy grinned. "Who is it?"

"You know dang well who it is, Clar-ay Black. It's Roads and Budrow. Are ya decent?"

Brandy went to the door. "Well, it could'a been one of them handsome ex-soldier boys who was here."

"They rode out three hours ago. Now can we come in, or should we just go to bed? I've decided what I'm going to do."

Brandy opened the door. "Yeah, we're decent. Come on in."

Granite came in with Budrow trailing behind, a red flush suffusing his face. "Howdy, girls."

Annette turned away. "Don't be giving us no 'howdy girls,' you two-timing snake-in-the-grass. You're just another claim-jumper with a handful of gimme and a mouth full of much obliged. Leave us in Colorado while you go off for a little fun and adventure. Two girls with broken hearts."

Nettie waded in. "Well, we ain't broken-hearted no more, Carson Budrow. You can go to hell in a handbasket as far as I'm concerned."

Granite stepped in between them. "Look, ladies, I'm sorry about us beating it out of town, but that's become a minor issue for me. I'm going after Alice and bringing her in. It's gotta be me. No one else can save my family's name. Budrow's coming with me."

"So am I," said Brandy.

"And me," said Nettie.

"And you're not leaving me behind again," said Annette.

Granite looked at the three women. "The hell you say."

Brandy stepped tight up in Granite's face. "The hell you don't say."

Granite looked at the three women. Not one of them was going to take water from him.

He looked at Budrow, who shrugged.

"Well, dang, ladies. I guess we got an outfit."

CHAPTER 3

QUANTRILL'S MEN

The ride through the town where Roads's sister had shot the lawmen changed nothing for Nettie or Claret. Despite talking to the mayor, the barkeep, and a mercantile owner—all of whom had seen Alice shoot the men dead—the two women still refused to believe it. Annette said nothing one way or the other. Roads went to the cemetery and to the graves. The others waited outside the gate. Then all five went to the saloon, had coffee on Budrow's dime, and moved on. Roads shrugged the group off and went ahead. He was in no hurry, but he plainly did not want company.

Budrow nudged his horse up alongside anyway. "Mad at the world?" he asked Roads.

Roads kept his eyes straight ahead, fixed on miles of Texas flatlands that spread in all directions. "I will not abide fools."

"Is that what the ladies are now? Fools? I thought you—"

Roads held up a gloved left hand. "I have my code, and I must abide by it. When people willfully ignore the evidence staring them in the face, I have no use for further talk. How many times did I see generals and colonels ignore the facts and send our men into slaughter? Lee, of all people, did it at Gettysburg, despite Longstreet's admonitions, and Pickett's men paid for it in spades on July 3rd. Shot to pieces. For nothing, Budrow, for nothing. Now we glamorize the butchery and say how gallant the Virginians were. It's insanity."

"What are your intentions?"

"If you are wondering why I am taking my time, it's because I know the gang my sister has attached herself to will do something else that raises eyebrows, giving me time enough to hurry to that location and track them from there. I will inquire in every town if there is more news. It won't be long."

"What about Nettie and Claret?"

"What about them? I told you. I will not indulge them in their folly."

"We can discuss—"

"There is nothing to discuss. It is not a member of their family who has cut the reins and became an outlaw. There is no blood debt for them to expiate. It is on *my* head. It is on *my* honor. I must set things right, Budrow. I must balance the books."

"Balance the books?"

"It is a bookkeeping metaphor I favor."

"I thought God Almighty kept the books."

"The Lord has his books to tend to. I have mine."

"The ladies think you're angry with them, Granite."

"I *am* angry with them, Kit."

"Is the entire ride going to be like this?" asked Budrow.

Roads grunted. "It depends."

"On what?"

"On whether any of them will squeeze the trigger when the time comes."

Roads did not share any campfire time with the other four that night or the night after. No one forced their company on him. Days in the saddle were quiet, though the other four talked, nights at the fire and in the bedroll quieter. They could see Roads smoking the small cigars or the cheroots he favored and sipping from a flask filled with bourbon. Every time they came upon a saloon, he made sure he replenished the silver flask. He was never drunk, just well-fortified as Budrow described his condition to the women.

They had been on the trail a little more than a week when they rode into a larger town where people were out in the street. Some racing about, some hollering, some saddling horses. Roads walked Sharpsburg up to a tall man with a pitchfork standing at the wide-open door to the livery.

"May I inquire what all this activity is about?" he asked.

The man barely glanced at him. "The Ten. It was for darn sure them. Robbed the bank, and it had a good stash. Cattle money." He shook his head. "And that woman was with them. Chica Bandida. I have no idea what her real name is."

"She was raised Alice Jeans Roads."

The livery man didn't skip a beat, only transferred his pitchfork from one hand to the other, glanced at Roads again, then back at the melee in front of them. Men emerged from the bank carrying a body draped in a white bedsheet. "She shot the bank manager dead," he told Roads. "Just for the hell of it."

"How do you know?"

"That's what the tellers told the posse. They aim to get her for the reward. Dead or alive."

"What is the count on the reward?"

"One thousand in silver. This here's the second posse just forming up. The first men were on the trail within fifteen minutes after the gang left town."

"If they are on them too quickly, there will be bloodshed."

"They are counting on that. They want Longhorn to go down as the town that ate The Ten alive."

"It may be the posse's bloodshed more than the gang's."

The livery man shook his head. "Not likely. Five of the men rode with Quantrill. They know how to put bullets where they do some good. I'd say The Ten and their woman are in for a beating."

Budrow was at Roads's left elbow.

"Did you hear?" Roads asked him.

"I did."

"I do not want others exacting a justice that falls to me."

"What are you going to do?"

"Befuddle the posse."

Roads urged his horse along the street and fell in behind the second posse as it galloped east. Once they were out of town, he gave them a wide berth and looped out of sight into a long strip of low-slung hills. From a knoll, he peppered the nine men with rapid Winchester fire, wounding several in the arms to show he meant business, praying they wouldn't bleed out before they got help. The posse turned back. Roads raced on ahead. He did not know where Budrow and the ladies were and didn't care. His mind was elsewhere.

He didn't push his gelding. He trotted Sharpsburg for a half-hour, walked for twenty, then rode slowly for another half-hour. He came upon the standoff he'd been hearing long before he spotted the men involved. There was a scramble of boulders, scrub, a creek, and men blasting away at one another from either side of the skinny run of water. One of the posse saw him and shot the heel off one of his boots. Then he put two bullets into Roads's butternut slouch and another across the back of his left hand. There was a bright squirt of blood, and the shot hurt worse than a horse kick to the shins.

Roads decided this made it easy to draw down on the posse—they were trying to kill him. He spurred Sharpsburg into his own pile of rocks, two of the men trying to pick him off, tucked the gelding out of sight along with himself, then began cracking rounds into the posse's backside with his Yellow Boy. They were caught in a crossfire. If they scrambled over the rocks away from Roads, a cluster of The Ten had them dead to rights. If they stayed where they were, backs to Roads, he could cut them up like stalks of corn. Roads poured in about a dozen bullets, then sat back and reloaded while shots pinged off the rocks around his head. Then cut loose with another ten shots and stopped. He wanted to give them a chance to light out. They did. All but one.

Sprayed by shots from The Ten, Roads watched the posse head back the way they'd come, hugging the backs of their horses, going full steam like a string of locomotives. Roads glanced at the creek between him and The Ten. It wound around the rocks and boulders and was a hundred feet from Roads. He hadn't given it one thought since he'd engaged the posse. When he heard a branch break, he instantly knew someone had crept up from the creek bank, and he spun with his Yellow Boy. A man leaped on him, smacked the barrel aside, punched Roads in the face hard, then wrapped his hands about Roads's throat.

"This is gonna do me good, bushwhacker," the man growled, cutting off Roads's breath. "Ain't killed a bad man this way since Appomattox. 'Course, he was a no good, ugly-as-sin, fiddleback, blue-belly Yankee, but a snake like you will do just as well." The man leaned into Roads, throwing as much of his body weight as he could down onto Roads's throat. "I'm gonna pop you like a cork and let you drain your mess into the mud."

Roads could reach his knife, but the man was still wearing his Confederate cavalryman's uniform, and Roads refused to kill him. The best he could manage, as his mind swirled in black and white and red rings, was to tug his blade free and slam the stag and steel pommel into the man's temple. Such a blow might kill the cavalryman, but it was the fastest method Roads could employ to stop him from ending Roads's life first. It took three strikes, as hard as Roads could muster with the portion of strength the strangling had left in him. The cavalryman sank on top of Roads and didn't move. Roads rolled him to the side and quickly felt under the man's gray jacket for his heartbeat. At first, he could feel nothing, and he swore. But on the third try, he felt the man's heart move and sat back, relieved. Until he heard a pistol cock.

"Had to find out who you were," a man said, "because I knew you weren't one of us."

He was lean as a blade of timothy, hairless, no beard, no hat. His Navy Six was pointed at Roads's head.

"Keep your hands just like that except drop the knife first," the man ordered Roads. "Good. Now, go ahead and tell me why you're helping us. You wanna join the gang or something?"

"I am looking for my sister," Roads replied.

"Your sister?"

"It's my understanding she is riding with you all."

"Ain't no woman riding with us, mister."

"Alice Jeans Roads. That is her maiden name. The newspapers call her La Chica Bandida."

The man stared at Roads for a moment, and then he roared. "Sure they do. She is our *vaquera*. What, man? You say she is your sister?"

"Yes. I need to speak with her."

"Speak with her? She's already spoken for, ha-ha. Our boss, Jack, has taken a liking to her. They will find a priest and do it up right when we don't have a posse breathing down our necks. Which you helped take care of. So, I'll make it short and sweet for you as a way of saying thanks. You won't know what hit you. Take it from me, *hombre*, the sister you knew and grew up with … she ain't that girl anymore. You wouldn't know her to see her. She is ice, man. A snake-eyed killer. Better you die remembering her the way she was. I swear to God, that is what I would want if this was my sister who was all full of hell. I'd want the memory of the good sister to take with me into eternity. This here is a gift I'm giving you."

The shot was followed by another shot. And another. And another. Four shots. None of them from the pistol of the lean, hairless man. But all the bullets were in him. He gave Roads a puzzled look. Then he toppled backwards, still gripping his Navy Six.

The shots had been taken from two hundred yards away. Maybe more. The shooter had slid his rifle over his saddle and fired. The horse hadn't flinched. Roads saw all that after the first shot hit home. He waited for a fifth shot for him. It didn't come. The man mounted and rode over at a fast trot. He looked down at Roads. He was wearing CSA gray like the man Roads had pounded senseless. The rifle wasn't pointed at Roads but a LeMat was. Nine rounds and a charge of buckshot that would flay Roads alive. The man smiled. He holstered the revolver.

"I know you're not with The Ten. And I know you're not with us. I don't know what happened with Teddy, but if you had to smack the bullheaded fool around, I'm sure you had your reasons. I don't know what cause you had to shoot at us, sir. But I know who you are. Granite Roads. Colonel Granite Roads. Welcome back to Texas."

CHAPTER 4

APPOMATTOX

"Do I know you, son?"

"Yes, sir. Don't you place me?"

Roads stared at the young man. Then it came to him. "Cooper?"

"Yes, sir."

Roads slowly got to his feet. "By dang. Last I saw of you was ..."

"Appomattox Courthouse, sir."

"At the surrender."

Both men were silent for a moment. Then Roads reached out and took the younger man's hand. "Coop, for goodness' sake. You weren't much more than a drummer boy the first time I saw you, back when Hood put the Texas Brigade together. But in those last fights in the Wilderness, Cold Harbor, and such ..."

"I remember, sir."

"You were as much of a man as a commander could ask for."

"And you were a genuine officer, Colonel. Not like those pantywaist rich boys who came over from Richmond with their fancy horses and plumed hats just in time for the end.

Sat there during the siege attending soirees and taking tea with the ladies while their men rotted in the trenches, then showing up in time to go home."

"Well, I wouldn't have been a colonel if the rest of the officer corps hadn't been wiped out. If you remember, they busted me down for insubordination at Gettysburg."

"But colonel, you were just standing with General Hood. He told Longstreet we shouldn't go after Little Round Top. But Longstreet wouldn't go against Lee."

"Well, Lee was wrong, and Longstreet was right. We should have slipped east with the entire army, got between Meade and Washington DC, found some high ground more to our liking, and been the ones holding the top of a hill when they came hightailing after us. But Lee sent Pickett two miles over open ground up that stinking Cemetery Ridge to the death of his division and the end of the Southern dream. Blast Lee and his Cause!"

There was a groan at their feet. Roads looked down. Roads's attacker was coming to. Granite pushed the burly would-be strangler with his toe. "And who's this friendly customer, Coop?"

"Teddy Wilkins. He's one of the men rode with Quantrill. An unsavory customer."

"Yes, I heard in town some of Quantrill's boys were with this posse. What's that about?"

"You know Quantrill got thrown out of the Reb army when he massacred everybody in Lawrence, Kansas?"

Roads nodded.

"Well, a bunch of his men headed out to Texas looking for greener pastures just a horse-fork ahead of a posse of angry Kansas citizens, unlike Jesse James and the Younger boys who started their own gang and kept on raiding down Kansas way after the war ended."

Wilkins tried to sit up but fell back down. He put his hand to his head. "Whaddya hit me with? A horseshoe?"

Roads grinned, and suddenly his Bowie was in his hand.

Cooper reached down and gave the man a hand up. "This is Colonel Roads of the Texas Brigade. You are lucky he didn't give you the business end of his Bowie."

"Well, how did I know? He was shootin' at us." He turned to Roads. "Why in tarnation was you doin' that?"

"Personal reasons, Mr. Wilkins. If I remember, you boys opened up on me first. You pay your money, and you take your choice."

"Well, I'll be remembering that thumping."

Granite slipped his knife back into its sheath and shifted his holster into business position. "Any time you want to address the grievance committee, Mr. Wilkins, we will be happy to accommodate you."

Wilkins's hand twitched, but he looked at Cooper, who smiled and slowly shook his head. "Would be a wrong move, Teddy. I've seen you draw. Before you could get your hawgleg out, the colonel would have three bullets in the tobacco pouch in your shirt pocket and you'd be shooting your toe off."

Wilkins's hand relaxed and dropped away from his gun.

Roads moved away to where the dead outlaw was lying. "Well, now that's settled, who's this owlhoot? Looks like they will have to call their gang The Nine."

Cooper studied the face. "I believe that's Jasper Jamison. He was a lounger around Longhorn for a while until he hooked up with The Ten."

"Well, let's ride over to them rocks and see what we can see. Where's your horse, Wilkins?"

"Over behind them rocks, Colonel."

Granite motioned with his hand. "Go fetch him and head back to town."

Wilkins grinned. "Well, Colonel, I think I will ride back to Longhorn, but I'll be fetchin' the rest of my boys. We got some Missouri trackers, and I reckon they will still be interested in that ree-ward. Besides, it seems like you're still going after them varmints, and you might need some help."

Granite looked at the man. "I'll tell you once, Wilkins. This is personal business, and I don't need any help. If you and your boys follow us, there will be trouble."

Wilkins spat and wiped his beard. "I guess you don't know who we are."

Granite bored the man with a piercing look. "I know who you are. Quantrill's Raiders—murderers, baby-killers, man-burners, and pond scum. You were a stain on the honor of the south. Quantrill got what he deserved when they shot him down in that Tennessee barn, and I reckon the good Lord has the same in mind for you and your pards. Now git!"

Wilkins scowled and walked away. Roads started heading toward the rocky hill where The Ten had holed up.

"Mind if I tag along, Colonel?"

"Don't you have a family around here, Coop, a wife? Last I saw you, back in Virginia, you had a picture of a sweet little thing you were fixin' to marry. What happened?"

Cooper pulled off his hat. "Cholera took her in '65 before I could get home. When I got here, her folks had pulled up stakes and left for California."

Granite put his hand on Cooper's shoulder. "I'm sorry to hear that, son. I know you set great store on that little gal. Nowhere else to call home, boy?"

"My mother has a place in Longhorn, but since I got back, I've been kind of at loose ends. If you don't mind, sir, I'd like to help. What's all this about?"

Granite pulled out a cheroot. He offered one to Cooper, who shook his head. Granite struck a match on his jeans as he took Sharpsburg's reins. "It's about my sister, Alice. She's gone to the bad. Shot her son and husband and joined up with The Ten. Now, I know something must have made her go over the edge, but she still needs to answer for her misdeeds. And I'm the only one with the right to see that happen. It's a matter of honor."

"But you aren't dealing with just your sister. You got ten ... I mean ... nine men, all mean as a grizzly mama with three cubs. Sure you don't need some help?"

Granite looked up. Four riders had appeared over a rise about a mile away. "You know, Coop, I just might. Those riders over there are my outfit. Carson Budrow and three ladies, two of whom were Lady Rangers before the carpetbaggers got here—Nettie Paris and Claret Brandy Black—tough as nails. The third is a little southern belle the west has taken holt of in a big way—Annette Devereaux. She carries a fifty-caliber pistol, and she shot some of Skin Ricketts's bushwhackers into ragdolls in a little set-to we had up near Denver."

Granite took a long drag. "But here's my problem, Coop. Two of those gals, Nettie and Claret, are real close friends with Alice, and they still haven't accepted she's crossed the line. So, they are riding under protest. Budrow, he's a good man, but he's neutral, as is Annette. I might need someone who will back my play without question. Can you do that?"

Cooper nodded. "I'm your man, Colonel."

"Good, Coop. Good."

★★★

Twenty minutes later, Budrow rode up followed by the ladies. Granite looked him over. "What took you so long?"

Budrow slid off Ranger and stretched his legs. "Well, you took off outta there like a branded calf, and I had to round up the ladies."

Nettie laughed. "You wouldn't know a lady if she was bitin' yer lip, Budrow."

Budrow turned. "You know, Nettie, you're right to ride me. I skunked out on you and Annette big time back there in Colorado. I admit I was wrong, and I apologize. Now, if we're gonna ride together, you don't have to be friendly, but I'd appreciate turning the vitriol down a few notches."

Brandy snickered. "There's a fifty-dollar word, Kit."

Granite turned to Cooper. "This here is Gregory Cooper—Coop, we call him. He rode with me all the way through the war. Started out as a snot-nosed private who could barely heft his rifle. Along the way, he turned into a man—a man I counted on. A man who shot Jasper Jamison four times from two hundred yards when the polecat had me boxed for sure. I asked him to ride along, seein's how his sweetheart is in heaven and his pa's been gone a long time."

Nettie spit and smiled. "You know we don't cotton to just anybody until we know how he stacks up. Can we ride the river with him? That's what I want to know."

Granite was about to speak when Cooper suddenly whipped out his .44 and fired into the ground right behind Nettie.

Nettie flamed red and went for her gun. Budrow put a hand on her arm and whispered. "Before you send him to his reward, you should probably take a look at the sidewinder that was a'comin' up on your backside."

Nettie turned. Sure enough, a big rattlesnake was flopping its death dance in the brush right behind Nettie. Only this snake didn't have a head. Nettie smiled and stuck out her hand.

"I reckon you'll do, Coop."

***

Carson Budrow stood watching the sun paint the gray dusty plain with orange strokes. Out to the west was a flat region with a poor growth of mesquite and prickly pear. The evening breeze picked up fine grains of sand and blew them down the hill. Their camp was a secluded spot under a grove of thick oaks. A small stream wandered down from the canyon above them, and it fanned out a little just beyond their camp into a small meadow of green grass surrounding a tiny pond where the picketed horses were eating their fill.

Some stars sparkled in the growing indigo above. A low range of hills lined the eastern horizon, and the fading light was creeping up their sides, moving from deep purple at the base of the hills to a ruby red along the ridge tops. Carson looked down at the camp. The girls were laughing around the fire, and some biscuits were browning in the Dutch oven. The smell of coffee floated up, and Budrow's mouth watered.

Cooper seemed to be a hit with the girls, and he was shyly accepting their attentions. Granite walked up the hill to where Budrow stood.

"Smoke?"

Budrow took a cheroot and lit it. "Why are you bringing this kid along, Granite?"

Granite took a long drag. "I need someone who will follow orders without hesitation. I can count on Coop." Granite saw the scowl on Budrow's face. "Look, Kit, I ain't saying I don't trust you. You and me are pards. I trust you with my life."

"Well, what are you saying, then?"

"I just don't know if I can trust you to shoot Alice if I need you to. That's because you're a gentleman—only one I've ever known. When the cards are laid on the table, and I say jump, Coop will jump."

Budrow took a drag and smiled. "You know me pretty good, Granite."

CHAPTER 5

LONGHORN

They went back to Longhorn for the night.

Roads had never been in a hurry to track the outlaws to begin with, and he saw no reason to hurry now because the gang's crimes would lead him right to his sister. He knew some might think he was dragging his heels because he truly had no interest in apprehending Alice. It was not true, but he knew his apparent reluctance to catch up with his sister would sit well with Nettie and Claret, possibly Budrow and Annette as well. Who knew? He did not expect anyone to be truthful with him except the new man, Cooper, who had no vested interest in Roads's sister.

Coop had made himself four hundred Yankee dollars for killing one of The Ten. While he pocketed most of it, he took the unusual step of making sure everyone in the group—none of whom he had known much longer than a day and a night—had a Winchester Yellowboy. He laughed off the surprise from Roads's band. "It's an investment in myself, y'all. It may be your shot from the Yellowboy that saves my skin." When Nettie said she'd already picked one up, he asked her what she'd like instead.

"Lord, you know my kind of candy and flowers." She roared and threw back her beautiful head with all its beautiful red hair, which for the moment, she'd unbound in anticipation of putting down twenty-five cents for a hot, sudsy bath. Roads saw the flash in Coop's eyes when he saw her beauty flare out from under her dusty wide-brimmed hat where she had buried it. Roads was aware Budrow saw the young man's fascination with Nettie's lovely fire.

"Let me have my bath, Coop," she told him, "and then I shall go down to the mercantile and see what they all have for sale."

She patted the young man's cheek with her bare hand. Roads and Budrow knew it would ignite a firestorm in Coop's soul, and they were confident Nettie knew it too. They could see her relishing Coop's confusion and excitement. She added fuel to the fire. "Meet me there at six if y'all like."

Nettie headed for her bath. She did not flinch from Budrow's perplexed gaze. "Every now and then a gal needs to kick up her heels to keep her feeling like a woman," she whispered. "Don't look so worried, Kit." Then she laughed like a nineteen-year-old, Roads thought. Good Lord above, what had gotten into her? Why was she bringing out her wild streak? He would find out a few hours later from Claret.

But later, Nettie had her bath and came out shining in a clean denim shirt and pants, her red hair a fire all down her back, bewitching Coop even more, and "every man and boy in Longhorn," Budrow growled, helpless to do anything about it. She picked out a Colt 1861 Navy Conversion in .38 caliber, center fire, pearl handles, and a tooled Slim-Jim holster to go with it, along with a couple hundred rounds of ammunition. She enjoyed Coop's fascination with her and let him hover and hum around her like a bee over red roses, her mischievous smile telling Roads she wanted Budrow to notice and hoped to play with his heart and soul too.

She coaxed a pearl-handled derringer out of Coop before the buying and selling was done, a pricy piece that had the shopkeeper glowing as the young cowboy spread out his cash on the counter. *On the counter*, Roads grunted to himself, *but literally at Nettie's feet.* Roads's new friend was besotted with the tough Texas beauty, and she added to Coop's romantic inebriation by giving him a kiss on the cheek this time. "Oh, Cooper, you are too sweet to me. But I like it." She looked for the darkness and turmoil in Budrow's eyes as he stood there, unable to stop her game, found it, and liked that too.

Claret came to Roads that evening and explained. She arrived at his room unannounced, all washed, pink, and fresh from her own hot bath, hair blazing like silver coins in the sun. She dropped into a chair beside his, leaned over and plucked the cigar from his lips, then placed it between her own with a saucy smile. She drew on it as she propped her boots on his arm, her skirt riding up just above her knees, blowing the smoke in his direction. "You haven't had much time for me lately, Garrett."

"Things have been hectic. As you know."

"Have you noticed I'm the only one who calls you Garrett? For some it's Granite. For others, it's just plain old Roads. For me, your childhood sweetheart you never could quite forget, it's your Christian name."

"What's going on, Claret?" He sipped at his glass of bourbon.

"What's going on? Well, let's see, let's start with Annette. We've talked her over to our way of thinking, Garrett."

They were in a large house set back from the town among acres of grass. It was Coop's house. His parents' house.

Though his father was gone, killed at Antietam, his mother still ran the roost, young enough, strong enough, and fiery enough to handle Coop, his two brothers, and three sisters, all of whom were over twenty. Mrs. Cooper, Athena, who had been a teen bride, wasn't a day over forty and looked thirty-five. Not to be argued with, boasting nerves and arms like iron, she'd insisted Roads and his four companions stay over at her home, where she swiftly gathered them in like family, fed them, made sure they were washed and their clothes laundered, and gave them all beds to sleep in. Roads and Budrow were together, but Claret had clearly waited till Budrow was out and gone before entering Roads's room and closing the door behind her.

Roads took a moment to think over what Claret had said about Annette going over to Claret's and Nettie's way of thinking. "How so?"

Claret grinned. "What do you think? She believes Alice is innocent and has joined forces with us to thwart your plans."

Roads curled his fingers. "This is my posse."

"Not anymore, Garrett. You've lost the vote in Congress and the Senate."

"I have Budrow and Coop."

Claret laughed, blowing tobacco smoke in his face. "You had Budrow and Coop. Where do you think your friends are now? Both of them are walking Nettie in the flower garden with all its lovely spring blossoms. Hopelessly contending for her affections. I believe the handsome widow Athena is accompanying them. Quite a little entourage. Budrow and Coop will do whatever Nettie tells them to do. Maybe even what the bold and beautiful Mrs. Cooper tells them as well. Which is to protect Alice from you, make sure she escapes, and keep her safe and alive."

Roads was so stunned he could not even feel anger. "I won't stand for it."

"Five of us against one of little old you? You have little choice. Actually six. Or more like eleven. Poor Roads. Worse odds than July 3rd at Gettysburg."

"What are you talking about?"

Claret leaned back in her chair and luxuriated in a long stretch, exhaling. She felt Roads's eyes riveted on her and smiled, aware he would always be hers, no matter what, and let her words out slowly and firmly. "You no longer run our band. Me and Nettie do. And the others have voted in our favor. Which includes the handsome widow and her children. Nettie and I have convinced them all. We save Alice, we keep her from you, we keep her from the hangman's noose, and above all, we keep her free of your twisted sense of Southern honor. Who hunts down their own sister, Garrett? We deal with what used to be The Ten, whittled down to nine. We split the reward, which is substantial, and set up here in Longhorn, with or without you. We give Alice a new life and a new identity. We give ourselves new lives. You too, if you want it. Just be aware we mean business, Garrett, my dear. You no longer tell me what to do. I tell you. And you listen. Understood, darling?"

"Claret—"

"Shush, my sweet. I'm not done. You need to know I will cut you down if you try to get in my way or the way of the plans Nettie and I have made. You cannot have Alice, you cannot touch her. She is not yours or the law's. She's under my protection, mine and Nettie's. You know I can outdraw you. Nettie and Annette can outshoot you. If necessary, I will pull on you if you make me, darling. So don't."

In a flash, Roads yanked his pistol from its holster. But hers was already pointed at his heart. "An obvious move,

Garrett. I saw that one coming all the way from the Alamo. Now put your gun on the floor."

"Claret—"

"Stop repeating my name. You're being annoying. Put the gun down."

Roads did as he was told.

Claret's eyes had narrowed to slits and turned a dark indigo blue. "You had no time for me all the way from Colorado to Texas. That's when I decided I was too young and full of juice to settle down with any man, including you. Then you made us track your sweet sister, even though Nettie and I were at odds with you. That's when I decided. Nettie and I both made up our minds. You would not rule us. Who gave you permission to do what you wanted with our lives, our guns, and our principles? So, from today, we take our lives back, we free Alice from her abductors, and we tell you what to do and when. Men have too often treated women as their property. Well, now we're treating you as ours."

"I can't believe Budrow would go along with this."

"It is hard to believe, isn't it? But Nettie will have her way with him, just as she will have her way with Cooper. This is our gang now, and they are our men. Nettie and I are the new chica bandidas. You work for us, Garrett. You work for me." She chuckled and got out of her chair, keeping her pistol on Roads. He saw she had Nettie's nine shot Le Mat with the under barrel that fired buckshot. Then she leaned over and kissed him on the lips, pressing the gun barrel tightly into his chest.

He wanted to push her away. He was confused, angry, and hurt, and wanted not to like the kiss. But he did. And he knew she knew he liked it. Claret pulled away finally, smiling down at him. "Sweet dreams, darlin'." Then she buffaloed him, smacking her pistol hard against the side of his head. Roads slumped in his chair. She took his glass of bourbon and drained it, leaving a little to drip over his head. "It's Claret's rules from now on, Colonel Roads. I trust you'll be my good soldier."

She ground her cigar out against his boot, picked up his pistol, and tucked it in her gun belt. She took the derringer she knew was in his vest pocket. Stripped him of his US Marshal's badge and three knives, including a massive Bowie and a dagger strapped onto the calf of his left leg. The dagger was so sharp she cut her finger and cursed Roads while she sucked the blood—"Doggone it, Garrett. You are one hot mess." Finally, she called out, finger still in her mouth. "Valentina! Come in and hogtie him! He's more than ready!"

A young woman in jeans and a blue cotton shirt, raven hair, and ice-blue eyes, came in with a lasso. She looked at Roads and noticed, "You sure did him up right, Miss Claret." Then she began wrapping the rope around Roads and his chair. Claret nodded, Le Mat holstered, hands on her hips, watching Valentina Cooper tie off her knots and stuff a red bandana in Roads's mouth, "I did, didn't I? I knew I could. I had no doubts about that. He's not so much as he thinks he is. Good work. We'll come and get him at breakfast."

***

Breakfast for Roads was having Mrs. Cooper, who looked just like her daughter Valentina with a few extra years and pounds—but not many—hold a cup of coffee to his mouth and a gun to his heart. "It's all right, Colonel," she kept saying. "You'll see, everything will work out for the best. I realize it's difficult for a man to follow women's orders.

But just do what we tell you and we'll all wind up well off with wagon loads of cash. And your sister will be happy and free in the bargain. In time, you'll change your mind about everything. We'll see to that."

"This is ridiculous, Mrs. Cooper," Roads fumed. "Let me go and no charges will be pressed. I have a US Marshal's badge."

"It's Athena." She laughed, letting some coffee spill down his shirt. "Oh, yes, a Yankee badge. That holds no water around here."

"Unbind me."

She patted his cheek in a motherly way. "You could be one of my own boys. And I'll treat you as such." She slapped him hard across the face. "Do as you're told, sir. Don't disobey me or the others. No backtalk. Shooting you dead and leaving your carcass for the foxes and coyotes would be easy. Listen to me now. I am a kindly soul. But my sons and daughters matter to me. Get in the way and I'll put you under the ground faster than Nettie or Claret would."

Athena returned to her warm smile, untied him, bound his wrists together, marched him to the outhouse, then made him mount his horse. The others were all in the saddle and waiting in the farmyard. Roads scarcely knew her other two sons, had only been introduced to them when he'd first arrived at their home. Of the three daughters, he only recognized the dark-haired, blue-eyed, bewitching Valentina, who smiled at him darkly from under a hat that was too big. Everyone looked shapeless in their long riding coats and dusters, even Nettie and Claret and Annette, all of whom paid no attention to him. There was only one cause for relief. Budrow was on his horse, without a gun belt, and his wrists roped together like Roads's. Budrow nudged his horse over. "The war was easier, Granite."

"By the good Lord, you are right. Thank you for throwing in with me, Budrow."

Budrow nodded, eyes gray and murky. "There was no other choice. Though I reckon now I will never marry Nettie Paris. Or my dear Annette. Her head is all full of their talk."

"Nor I, Claret Black. I confess I still do not quite grasp all this. My head spins."

Budrow shrugged. "For Nettie, Claret, and Annette too, it's about being in charge of their own destinies—that's how they see it—and being in a position to ensure Alice's life and liberty. For the Coopers? The carrot is money. Lots of it. And not just the reward money."

Roads stared. "What do you mean?"

"I'm just saying Mrs. Cooper may have blue eyes that twinkle in the dark, black hair as shiny as a good night in the hill country, and a smile as sweet as hot biscuits and butter, but she is a force to be reckoned with, Granite. Her heart is nothing less than the hard steel of a bayonet, poised to run some poor devil through. I swear to it. Given the necessity, she would turn outlaw on a dime and take her children with her."

"What? Banks? Trains? Raids?"

"Any of it. That's my impression of her."

"Kit, what kind of hornet's nest have we pitched ourselves into here in Longhorn?"

Just then, Coop rode up and interrupted them. He shoved a scrap of paper into each of their bound hands. He would not look Roads in the face. "This here is a list of the names of all the outlaws we're tracking, plus some physical descriptions from the wanted posters. Lock all this up in your head. These are the men that need to die. We want Alice freed and the money due to us for the outlaws. That's all."

"Look at me, Coop," Roads demanded. "Have you lost your mind? You'd do this to a fellow countryman, a cavalry officer of the Confederacy?"

Coop kept his eyes averted. "I wouldn't have thrown in. But Mama insisted. I can't go against Mama. You know the commandments, Colonel. And then there's holy matrimony to think about—the opportunity to marry Nettie Paris."

"Is that what Nettie told you?" Roads flared. "What if my sister has become a killer, Coop? What about that?"

Coop shook his head. "I've been assured she can't be. And Mama believes that to be the case as well. My duty is clear. It's not to you, Colonel, or to the Confederacy. It's to family. That's the way my honor lies." Coop reined away. "If y'all try to escape, we won't chase you. Just shoot you down. Understand that. No warning shots. Just lead in the back."

The party walked their horses out of Longhorn by a back trail. Nettie, Claret, Annette, and Athena were in the lead. Valentina and a sister with straw-blonde hair stuffed under her hat brought up the rear. When Roads glanced back at them, they both smiled. The blonde patted the shotgun she held across her saddle.

"I hope you try something, mister," she said. "I been itchin' to trigger this bulldog on a man."

"Her name is Stella," Valentina explained. "She don't mean it. We'd just as soon be your fancy gals and marry ya'll as gun ya down."

Stella snorted and grinned. She had a gap-toothed smile and a million freckles around her blazing green eyes. "O' course, I mean it. Love a man, shoot a man, either will do."

"She don't mean it," Valentina repeated. "She'd rather raise a family with y'all. Fourteen or fifteen would be just about right. You say, Stella?"

Stella relented. "All right. Gimme the Yankee, and I'll teach him Southern ways proper. He's cute. Sixteen and a marriage."

Valentina fixed Roads with her ice and snow blue-sky eyes. But her smile was full of fire. "And I'll take you, Mister Granite, sir. A nice, handsome war hero for me. We'd have a good life. I guarantee it. Just don't spoil it by trying to get away. I won the last shooting contest in Longhorn. Twenty dollars prize money. Keep that in mind, war hero, sir, and keep your handsome head on those nice broad shoulders for me. I got plans for us two." She laughed the moment Roads looked away. "That rattled him some, Stella. I reckon he knows I hold his life in the palm of my hand. All of it."

Stella laughed with her. "I reckon they both know it. Betcha' I could take that Yankee in a horse race and a wrestle."

"You might hurt him."

"I wouldn't give him too bad a licking."

Roads ignored their bantering and stared at the paper Coop had thrust between his fingers. *Todd and Bishop Yancey. Sammy and Ferrell Kincaid. Pitch and Buddy Conner. Jesus Ramirez. Mateo Gonzalez. Diego Villa.* The names meant nothing. He looked over the scribble about hair color, height, eyes, scars. All of that meant even less. He wondered if he'd even get a shot off at any of them or whether he'd just wind up watching Nettie, Claret, Annette, and the Cooper family blow the outlaws out of their saddles. Or whether a scrawny straw-blonde with a shotgun might blow him out of his.

"A heck of a thing," Budrow muttered. "A heck of a mess."

Roads nodded. "It is. And no easy way to untangle the rope Claret and Nettie have tied us with. They laid their plans slick and strong and neither of us the wiser. The two of them played us for fools and happily watched us fall for everything, even Coop's cozy old house and his sweet, kind, smiling old mother."

"I don't just mean that."

"Then what do you mean? Valentina and Stella and their shotguns?"

"Not even that. We've got a lot more to think about." Budrow jerked his head to the side. "The Quantrill boys are following us. I expect they want the reward for the outlaws for themselves. Which means they'd kill everyone here. What we have to figure out—do we wind up siding with them and shooting ourselves free of this bunch? Including Nettie, Claret, and Annette? Or do we side with our gals and plant the Quantrills in the ground when the time comes?"

Roads grunted and glanced to the right like Budrow, catching a quick glimpse of a horse and rider. The rider wore a tattered gray uniform.

"They're hardly our gals anymore, are they, Budrow?"

CHAPTER 6

BIG BEND

They had been riding since before dawn. Budrow felt the rising sun warming his back. Ahead of him stretched a vast wild region of sparse grass, mesquite, and cactus. They had been traveling west for three days, and after the second night, the ladies had agreed to take the ropes off if they behaved themselves. Now Budrow and Granite rode ahead of the grim-faced women who had so unceremoniously usurped their command.

"What is this country, Granite?"

Roads took a pull on his cheroot. "Called the Big Bend country. It's all of Texas west of the Pecos." He pointed off to the right. "Up north there is the Llano Estacado. We rode by it after I saved you from Scarface Ragland and his boys. Nothing but shifting sands and cactus up there, not a drop of water for three hundred miles. I heard the boys back in Washington are planning to push a southern transcontinental railway through south of the plains, but it will be a few years until they get it going."

"Why the Big Bend?"

"The Rio Grande comes out of Colorado and hits Texas at El Paso. Then it flows due south along the border between

Texas and Mexico for a thousand miles. Somewhere out there …" he pointed his cheroot, "… it makes a left turn and heads north, a big bend. So, all the country held in that meander is called the Big Bend Country. Down in the south, it looks like a desert, but if you put water on it, the grass grows. Ranchers are pushing cattle in there, and pioneers are moving in, looking for a piece of land. There's one problem, though."

"What's that?"

"There's no law out there, so every hombre on the dodge in Texas ends up in Big Bend. See those hills out there?"

Budrow followed Granite's pointing hand. A line of hills showed themselves along the western horizon. The morning sun lit the tops with flashes of gold and pink.

"Yep."

"Those are the Ord Mountains. They wall off the whole western section of Texas. Up in them hills are some fancy hideouts. I imagine our boys and Alice are headed there. If we don't catch them before they get there, we'll have the devil's own time digging them out."

"Yeah, if we even get there. Looks like our early departure didn't fool the Quantrill boys."

Granite turned in the saddle. Sharpsburg snorted at the shift in weight. Behind them, about five miles back, he could see a faint cloud of dust rising over the bleak landscape.

"Not too far back but not pushing us. I think they are a little timid about facing so many guns."

Claret rode up from behind them.

Granite flicked his cheroot under her horse's hooves. "Howdy, Brandy Black."

Claret looked at him sideways. "Been a long time since you called me Brandy. I thought you liked Claret better."

"Well, I reckon I haven't seen Claret around since Longhorn. Just hard-nosed ol' Brandy, who's got no use for men."

Claret's face hardened, but not her eyes. Budrow could see a stab of hurt flash through them. Claret reached for Granite's arm but stopped. "What do you suggest we do about Quantrill's men? They're on us like stink on a hog."

Granite shrugged. "Makes no never-mind to me. You're the boss. Just make sure me and Kit have a couple of rifles when they come down on us."

Claret wheeled her horse and headed back toward the gang of women, plus Cooper.

"Well, that stuck in her craw, Roads."

"Can't stand the heat, don't play in Roads's kitchen."

★★★

In the afternoon, they saw Ord Mountain rising in front of them. Off to either side, the bleak peaks of Elephant Mount and Cathedral Mount stood as silent sentinels. More than any other part of Texas, the Big Bend country seemed to be a world to itself. They had passed a few ranches down in the more verdant valleys, and the ranges were thick with cattle.

They rode slowly into the small town of Marathon, a typical west Texas town. There were a few houses on the outskirts, and a main street featured a bank, a saloon, and a ramshackle hotel.

Roads swung down off Sharpsburg. "This is the gateway to rustler country, Budrow. Up in those hills are some of the toughest gangs in the west. This is the only settlement in this entire area. The ranchers who have moved in are getting rich, but the rustlers are getting richer. I'm thinkin' our boys are looking to join up with Cheseldine or one of the other rustler kings. We need to smoke them out before they disappear into one of these hidden valleys."

Nettie, Claret, Annette, and the Coopers rode up. Nettie dismounted and walked up the stairs to the porch of the saloon. A few idlers stared at the band of tough-looking women. One of them, obviously too drunk to see his danger, staggered up to Nettie and took hold of her arm. Before he could finish saying "Ain't you a pretty little thing," he was lying stretched out cold on the wooden walkway with blood running down his forehead and Nettie standing over him with her new Navy Colt in her hand.

"Any more of you fools want to get fresh?"

The look in her emerald-green eyes backed by the flaming-red hair falling to her shoulders gave pause to the locals.

"Sorry, lady. Jimmy didn't know."

Nettie moved over to face the group. Claret and Annette got down and stood behind her. The Cooper girls made sure their shotguns were clearly visible.

"Yeah, that's the way of men who don't have honor. Sittin' around in the saloon in an owlhoot town, getting drunk in the middle of the day. Thinkin' any woman who passes your way is fair game for your loathsome charms. Well, the part of Texas I come from hangs men for touching a woman or insultin' her."

Suddenly, Claret's Colt and Annette's .50 caliber were in their hands.

Claret grinned. "Or shoots 'em."

Nettie slid her pistol into its holster and pulled the makin's from her pocket. While she rolled a smoke, she looked at the men. "As far as I know, this is still Texas. Maybe you men ought to remember your mothers and sisters and your good, honest fathers scratchin' out a livin' in poor ground. That ought to make you ashamed of the life you're living."

The idlers, thoroughly cowed by now, began removing their hats and touchin' their foreheads. One of them, a dark-haired lad with a missing tooth, shuffled forward.

"You're right, ma'am. My ma would whup me good if she see'd how I'm livin'. I'm going back on this crowd and hauling my freight home. Don't know why I left." He turned away and walked down the street. A few of the others grumbled, but the crowd broke up, and soon they were standing alone on the boardwalk.

Budrow grinned at Nettie. "Well, from Ranger to drover to kidnapper to preacher. You have many facets, my dear Nettie."

Cooper spoke up. "Now, don't be giving Nettie a hard time ..."

Before he could finish, Ranger was right up against Cooper's horse, and Budrow had the young man by the shirt front.

"Now, I'm going to tell you something, youngster. My business with Nettie is my business and none of yours. You think you can waltz in with a handful of gimme and a mouthful of much obliged and win the fair maiden's hand. Now, I'm willing to let your stupidity pass, but if you want to start the ball, let's go."

Cooper's face turned red, and he reached for his gun. But suddenly, his mother was gripping his hand firmly.

"Now, Cooper, I didn't raise no stupid children. I've seen you draw, and I've seen Mr. Budrow draw, and you'd be shooting the dirt in front of your feet while he was putting two nice round holes in the front of your clean shirt. Now you apologize. Mr. Budrow is right. What he has to say to

Miss Nettie is none of your business. I'd advise you to keep your nose out."

The red in Cooper's face turned white as he looked back at Budrow and saw a gun in his hand where there had been none before. He moved his hand slowly away from his gun belt.

"Mother's right. I apologize, Mr. Budrow. I shouldn't have put my oar in."

Budrow smiled. "Apology accepted. Now, we should probably go find a place to camp—preferably outside of town and preferably hidden."

Roads swung back up on Sharpsburg, and he and Budrow led the way out of town.

"You wouldn't have shot him, would you, Budrow?"

"I would have."

★★★

Later that night, as Budrow and Roads were sitting by their fire away from the rest, Nettie, Claret, and Annette walked up.

Roads bit the end of his cheroot and spit it off into the darkness. "Howdy, Brandy. What can we do for you?"

"Well, you can call me Claret."

Roads stroked his mustache for a minute. "Claret Black is my friend. Brandy Black is not my friend. When you start behavin' like a friend, I'll call you Claret."

Nettie stepped in. "That's what we came to talk to you about. We want to make a deal that can get us back on the right foot."

Budrow looked at Nettie. She looked beautiful, but then so did Annette. "What's the deal, Nettie?"

Nettie looked past Budrow for a minute, then fastened her green eyes on his. "We realized, tough as we may be, we

50

don't have what it takes to lead this posse. We want to turn it back over to you two, but on one condition. Well, actually two conditions."

"What are they?"

"First is for Granite. We'll give the lead back to you if you promise to let the law deal with Alice once we catch up with her. I know you have your honor, and you feel this is a personal matter, but it's not. Every story has two sides, and we haven't heard Alice's yet. We're willing to take her in and let her make her case before a judge and a jury of her peers, legal and fair, and if the law hangs her, then so be it. But you are not to harm her—just help us find her. Can you agree with those terms?"

Granite looked at the women for a long time. He took a drag on his stogie, then nodded. "Okay, I'll agree. But what me and Kit say goes."

Annette smiled. "Well, that depends on Captain Budrow, and to some degree, you."

"What do you mean?"

"We women have realized there's just too much going on between the men and the women in this posse for us to keep our stories straight. We want to go back to the status we had before we met y'all. All bets are off, all promises canceled. We're just a bunch of folks out to right some wrongs, and we put the relationship angle on hold. Each of us is free to pursue our interests at a later date. But for now, we concentrate on getting the Quantrill boys off our backs and finding Alice."

Budrow spoke up. "What about Cooper and his overweening fascination with Major Paris?"

Annette grinned. "Do you blame him?"

Budrow shook his head. "Can't say as I do."

Nettie looked at Budrow. "I've warned him off, Kit. When I saw you were ready to kill him today, it set me to thinking. I don't need to be pitting the men against each other. That's not fair. From now on until we get this Alice thing settled, I'm just Major Paris, rider of the plains and very single."

"What about you, Annette? You can be a wicked enticer. You gonna put that part on ice?"

Annette curtsied. "Yes, my captain. Nettie and I have our own agreement ... which is none of your business. But I'll be good as gold. My .50 is the only thing sharing my dreams."

"What about the Coopers?"

Claret spoke up, "That's kind of the unknown quantity in this here mess. Athena Cooper has a lot going on in that brain of hers, and I don't think it includes going back to running a boarding house in Longhorn. She's got her eye on the reward, and she'll do anything to get it. And her kids will follow her without hesitation."

Granite shook his head. "Well, I certainly don't want to draw down on them girls. Can you ladies keep that pot from boiling until we get this sorted out? They can have my share of the reward. That's not what I'm after."

"Mine too," Budrow nodded.

Nettie smiled. "Is it a deal, then?"

Granite stepped forward and took Claret's hand. "It's a deal, Claret."

Claret smiled and blushed.

Budrow nodded. "It's a deal."

Just then, two rifle shots rang out, followed by the roar of a shotgun and pistol fire.

Granite and Budrow grabbed their rifles and ran down to the main campfire. Athena and the girls were not to be seen. Cooper came running into camp. "Two of Quantrill's boys snuck up. Valentina was on guard, and they didn't see her. She shotgunned one fella's arm off and he's done for. But Stella took a bullet, and Mam is looking after her. The other fella hauled his freight."

Granite looked at Cooper. "Get your gals in here. We need to break camp and ride before the rest of them come back." He looked at the others. "Knock those fires down and move."

CHAPTER 7

ATHENA'S BOAST

They spread out in the dark and crouched, guns ready.

Roads knew he could count on Nettie, Claret, and Annette to do their part. Coop too, much as he despised the young man. He brought all of them to mind and evaluated them, as he had done with his troopers during the war before any action took place.

Coop's mother, Athena, was tough as a keg of nails. She would give an excellent account of herself. Stella was patched up and held her shotgun as if she'd never been wounded. The other girl, Betsy, sixteen, another raven-hair like her mother, was taller than her siblings, even Coop and his brother, and looked to be made of bricks. She did not talk much, did not smile much. But she carried a Winchester Yellowboy with authority. As for Coop's younger brother, Seth, he was an unknown quantity. Fourteen and skinny as a whip, blond like Stella, but with strange eyes. Too bright, too many colors, never at rest, he reminded Roads of a wild pony he'd never been able to tame.

They waited a long time. They waited all night.

Nothing happened.

Come dawn, Roads, Budrow and Coop watched over the others while they got their sleep. Four hours. Coop was designated to drag the dead Quantrill off so they didn't smell him and to let the vultures have their breakfast. Then the three men got their sleep while the others watched. About noon, the entire party had coffee and bread as hard as a rock and rode on. That night, they camped again. Athena's children gathered up brush and deadwood, and she built a sizeable fire, making beans and coffee over it.

Roads took issue with the night fire being larger than he felt was safe. "This is too much. Altogether too much."

The others stood or sat around the flames. No one answered him but Athena. She snorted and mocked. "Are you afraid, sir? Do your knees knock together? It is no wonder we lost the war when we had officers like you. The fire is just right, not too large, not too cold. Do you think those Quantrill boys do not know where we are? They follow us night and day. Having no fire or a small one, too small to do us any good for cooking or warmth, does not keep us hidden. They are here."

Roads nodded. "I know they are here, Mrs. Cooper. I know they watch us. I know they decided last night was a mistake. If we're dead, who will lead them to Alice? They will have reconsidered, possibly pistol-whipped the attacker who survived, and will do little to harm us until we bring them to the prize—my sister. She is wealth to them."

"A good two thousand last I heard. Almost three. But it climbs the more damage she does and the more businessmen who contribute to the reward."

"That would be the way of it so long as the newspapers keep her legend alive."

"Right now, sir, my concern is the Quantrill boys. They are all our concern. I don't think we ought to wait until they do what they plan to do to us. If you find the courage, we should deal with them tomorrow or the day after. If you no longer have the courage, no matter. I have it. The women have it. My children have it. You are not needed."

"I have the courage, ma'am. Never fear."

"Do you? Do you look forward to putting an end to them as much as I do?"

Athena grinned and tossed another piece of brushwood on the fire. It flared up, igniting her face, making it, Roads thought, hideous. He looked away.

"Are you afraid of me, Roads? The good Lord knows you would not last one minute against me—knives or bare hands. I will have the Quantrill boys' blood and guts. I look forward to that. It is good to kill when the cause is right. Is it not? Didn't you kill scores of Yankees for the cause of a free Texas and a free Confederacy?" She brought a burning stick close to Roads's face, still grinning, taunting him. "Just remember, Mister High and Mighty, others may have decided to untie you, but you're not running the show anymore. It's me, Nettie, Annette, and Miz Black who say what goes. Why, even my girls are the boss of you. If you need a reminder, we'd be happy to kick some sense into you once more. Oh, we can do it. We've already done it. Some man and officer you proved yourself to be. Miz Black took you like she'd take taffy from a child. And if you don't like the fire, you can eat your beans and salt pork cold."

Which is exactly what Roads did, walking far away from the fire to sit with his back against a boulder, his plate in his lap. Budrow joined him after a few minutes, bringing his own tin plate letting off steam in the dark. They ate in silence for a while. Then Budrow spoke up.

"How long is this going to go on?" he asked.

Roads spooned up some beans, chewed, and swallowed. "I will not be ordered about. I am no schoolboy to be given lessons to. As for Miz Black, as Athena Cooper calls her, it is safe to say it is over between us, if there ever was anything on solid footing between the woman and myself."

"Granite, don't let your pride blind you, just because a woman bested you. She is strong. As many women are."

"Sometimes, Budrow, all we have left to live on is our pride."

"You know Claret still cares for you."

"She cares for my sister, and that is commendable. What she will do if my sister draws down on me remains to be seen."

"You know none of our women here think she is the bloodthirsty desperado the newspapers make her out to be," Budrow reminded him.

Roads nodded. "I'm aware of that. It does not mean they are right. They don't have a lifetime with her to go on like I do."

"Before I forget, this coffee is yours. I had mine back at the fire."

"Thank you kindly, sir." Roads took the tin mug, still steaming, and sipped it. "How are you and Nettie?"

Budrow shrugged. "We'll patch things up."

"I salute you." Roads lifted the tin mug. "But as you may surmise, I've lost interest in pursuing any sort of romance with Miz Black."

"No chance of a change of heart?"

Roads drank more coffee. "Doubtful. Let me say this, and I don't mind if you share it, as I have little to say in a personal way to any of the ladies who are on this trail with us. Alice had a mild disposition overall. She was a kindly soul. But if something stuck in her craw, Lord Almighty, it was stuck. She could blaze up like a prairie fire. I swear, she'd eat you alive. Do wild things, then come to her senses later. Why, she beat up a peddler once, sir. She took offense to his sass when she confronted him regarding one of his products she'd bought and found useless. She was only seventeen, Budrow, but she flattened him with two punches and was swiftly astride him, hammering him into the ground with her fists. I had to pry her off the unfortunate soul. She even talked about getting a musket. Took her an hour or two to cool off. Once she did, she was ashamed and repentant. Of course, the peddler had skedaddled and was long gone. A wise man. I persuaded her not to ride after him to make her apology. But I have seen her hold a grudge for months, Budrow, simmering like chili on a stove. Even a year once, blood was in her eye when she saw the man at church or heard his name mentioned. So, the ladies know nothing about the flip side of her coin. They may know heads. They know nothing about the reverse. Could she be wild enough to kill? Yes, indeed, Budrow, yes, indeed. That is why I must find her and put a stop to whatever is going on. I am responsible for her. The women are not. And they don't know two hoots about her."

Budrow waited a moment. "I found a page from a newspaper stuck on a bush. I did not show it to you."

"When?"

"Just this evening. Athena used a scrap of it to get the cook fire going."

"How old is it?"

"Nine days."

Roads grunted. "Could easily have been The Ten who lost it." He set down his empty mug and plate and glanced at a shooting star. He kept his eyes fixed there long after it was gone. "You'd best tell me what you didn't want to tell me, Budrow."

"Granite, you know these eastern papers. If they can make a story bigger and more sensational than it is to drive up sales, they'll do it. Now that they've made your sister into the devil herself, they have to print everything they hear even if it's lean on facts."

"Do you have that page on you?"

"It's in my pocket."

"I should like to see it. That will spare you having to tell me what she's done."

"What they *say* she's done."

Roads extended his hand as Budrow dug the folded over newspaper page from his pocket. Roads took the paper and opened the folds. He lit a small cigar, puffed till the tip was bright red, and used it to read by, careful not to ignite the paper.

There was a drawing of Alice rearing her horse and brandishing a smoking pistol in one hand. She wore a flat-brimmed, flat-crowned Spanish hat Roads always referred to as a bolero, though he'd heard the style called other names. The paper said a stage had been apprehended, its strong box and passengers looted. The driver and the guard had been shot and killed ... by Alice—Chica Bandida.

The passengers identified her. She didn't wear a mask. One passenger told the reporter she'd boasted she didn't require one because she had nothing to hide, since she claimed she only killed in self-defense. "Like any woman or man in Texas would do," was the quote.

Roads set the page down, leaned back against the boulder, and smoked the slim cigar.

"There is another shooting star," he announced. "That is unusual. Two in one night. What do you think it portends, Budrow?"

"I did not see it."

"But I did." Roads blew out a stream of smoke. "To change the subject completely, I own that I am weary of being trailed by the Quantrill boys. You may inform Miz Black, Annette, and Nettie that they are welcome to hunt them down with me tonight. The Coopers can guard the camp. They will not have to guard it from much. We will kill Quantrills within the hour. Oh, and invite Valentina along. She is an excellent shot."

Budrow stared at him. "We don't know where they are, Granite. And it's dark as tar."

"I am aware of the darkness, sir. It generally appears every day about this time. And we surely know where they are, Billy Yank. We've been watching them follow us for some time. But more to the point, the second shooting star was someone absentmindedly striking a match. It was a brief mistake, quickly smothered. I will come in from behind that spot." Roads ground his cheroot out on his boot. "I must reacquire my night vision. After you bring the ladies away from the fire, all of you will have to do the same. I am on the hunt in fifteen minutes. This will be short, sharp, and nasty, but worth the effort to get them off our backs."

"A night action? You are determined on that?"

"I am. There is no better time for invisibility. There are not above a dozen of the Quantrill boys. The ladies will make quick work of them. We will lend our assistance to the brave, bold Texan belles. And you might as well bring Athena along. She will not be denied her pound of flesh. That is the sort of person she is."

CHAPTER 8

SCRATCHIN' SOME FLEAS

Budrow slipped like a ghost through the dry chaparral that surrounded the Quantrill boys' campsite. The sparse dry grass of the Big Bend country softened the fall of iron-shod hooves. Budrow's thoughts went back to the night raids in Georgia as the Union Army under Sherman forced John Bell Hood's desperate ragtag army toward Atlanta. Budrow's boys were in the saddle day and night, pushing the tired Rebs, not giving them any rest. And now they were about to take the same action against the ex-raiders who had followed them from Longhorn.

To his left, Roads moved quietly. To his right, the women spread out in a circle around the camp. The guard whose unthinking match flare had allowed Roads to spot him had been quietly neutralized and now lay bound and silenced. The gray light of dawn was just breaking up the early morning darkness when Roads lifted his hand. The encirclement was complete. Roads eased through the last wall of brush and stepped out into the open. The men lay sleeping around the cold campfire, unlike Athena's blaze announcing to the world where the Roads outfit camped, had been built under a rock outcropping with dry wood that would not smoke.

Sharpsburg's hoof rang on an upturned stone and two of the more alert men in the ragged gray uniforms sat bolt upright, scrambling for their pistols.

"I wouldn't do that if I were you."

Roads's quiet voice and the big colt revolver in his hand stopped their frantic searching. They quieted even more when Budrow appeared, followed by Athena, Nettie, Annette, and Claret.

The one Budrow assumed to be the leader spoke up. "Well, Roads, looks like you got us."

He stood up, but then his hand moved toward the ground.

"Gun!" shouted Athena, and the roar of her 10 gauge revolving shotgun followed the shout. Before Roads could stop her, Athena shot down three of the men, two still in their blankets.

"Don't shoot, don't shoot. I'm out of it."

The fourth man turned to run, and at the same time pulled a pistol from his waistband. He started to toss it away, but before he did, he was met with a blast from Claret's Henry rifle. Nettie and Annette's guns were in their hands, flames spouting. The raider jerked backwards like he had hit the end of a lariat and flew into a cholla. He screamed as the deadly needles pierced through him, and he writhed and jerked. Athena pulled off the last round in her shotgun. The man jerked again, and then he died. His eyes stared at them as he hung there in the cactus tree.

Athena laughed. "He looks like he just got crucified. Wonder if he's going to heaven, like the thief on the cross." She laughed again.

Budrow looked at the woman. She had a glaze in her eyes and a grin on her face. "Well, we got no more trouble from those varmints, and now, we can get on after the reward," she said.

Roads dismounted and walked over to the bodies of the dead men. He knelt and stripped off the blankets. Then he looked up at Athena, a grim set to his mouth.

"These men were not armed. You had no call to shoot them."

"No call? No call? First of all, how was I to know they didn't have guns under them blankets? And second, they was bothersome. If we didn't kill them first, they would have snuck up on us and killed us like dogs. Now, we don't have to worry. We can make the main thing the main thing."

Roads walked over to the woman. "You know what? They wouldn't have killed us. Not before we tracked Alice down. I was planning on setting them afoot and letting them make their way back to the last settlement. You're a skunk in woman's clothing. You have no honor. You're just as bad as one of those saloon women who sell themselves to all the men who come along. Kill for money? You're sick. You and your brats best be gone by the time the sun is at mid-heaven. And take your treacherous son with you."

Athena bristled. "Call me a whore, will you? Why ... you don't tell me nothin'. Like I said, you ain't runnin' the show no more ..."

As she spoke, she swung her shotgun toward Roads. Before she could bring it to bear, Roads lashed out like a striking rattler. His fist connected solidly with her chin, and she went down without a sound. Roads looked up at the three women.

"Brandy Black! Nettie! You should be ashamed of yourself. That man was throwing his gun away, and you shot him down like a dog. You women used to be Rangers. What's happened to you?" Garrett pulled the blankets up over the faces of the dead men.

"These men may have been skunks, but they were Confederate soldiers at one time and fought for the Cause. They deserved a better death than this." He gestured down at the unconscious Athena. "Well, you can wait here with this fool and then ride with her when she wakes up. That won't be for several hours, so that'll give me a head start. But I'm telling you right now, Miz Black. If we cross paths down the road, and I find you interfering with me and my business with Alice, I'll shoot you where you stand."

Claret's face went white.

"And you other two. You can ride where you want, but it's not with me. And what I said to Miz Black goes for both of you. You ride with her, you interfere, and I'll give you the same treatment."

"You'd shoot us, Garrett?" Nettie's eyes went wide.

Claret saw steel come into Roads's face. "In a heartbeat, Nettie Paris, if you get in my way. As for our deal back there in the camp, all bets are off. After what I've seen here tonight, I have no interest in riding with a bunch of women who let power go to their heads and shoot down unarmed men."

He turned to Budrow. "Your call, Kit."

Budrow shook his head. "Roads is right. What was done here tonight is something a lowdown skunk would pull. You want to ride with the Coopers, you're more than welcome. But let me give you a word of advice. That woman lying there is pure poison. She's after the reward, and she'll do anything to get it. And if you get in her way, she won't hesitate to kill you. I predict by the end of all this she'll be riding the outlaw trail, and if you stay with her, you'll be no better than Alice. Me, I'm riding the Honor Trail with Roads." He jerked a thumb back toward their camp. "We're gonna set the guard free, give him water and a pistol, and point him east. He better get to where he's goin' alive. And as for these men, there's a shovel back in the wagon. You can bury them proper—like Texans do—or ride out, whatever suits your little fancies. But when you finish, don't be riding after us. Might get a little hot."

Nettie stretched out her hand. "Kit ..."

"Go on, Nettie. You can ride with young Cooper and twist him around your finger. And the name is Carson. My friends call me Kit. Let's ride, Granite."

Roads swung up on Sharpsburg, and the two men turned and rode off into the dawn, leaving three thoroughly chastised and very surprised women behind them.

★★★

By noon, Budrow and Roads were deep in the Ord Mountains. This section of Texas was a world unto itself. Between two of the largest peaks was a pass into the heart of this outlaw-infested region. At the mouth of this pass was a little village, the town of Ord, named after the largest of the peaks that loomed off to the south.

Granite gave Budrow a word of advice as they rode down the dusty street toward the only saloon in town. "Like I told you, ranchers and settlers have been coming in here, and the herds are growing. But Ord is also a den of thieves. When we go in there, half the men will probably be outlaws and half honest riders. One of these days, the law will get here, but until then, we're our own law. So follow my lead."

They loose-hitched their horses at the rail, walked up the steps and through the swinging doors. Inside, it was dark and smelled of smoke, whiskey, and sweat. There were a few tables scattered around the room where grim-faced men sat playing cards. Roads and Budrow stepped up to the bar.

The bartender wiped the counter clean in front of them with a dirty rag. "Howdy, gents, what'll it be?"

Roads nodded. "Rye, two glasses, and leave the bottle."

Budrow and Roads watched the action in the room. There were the usual cowhands, a few tough-looking quiet types, and two flamboyant bar girls cadging drinks. Budrow nudged Roads and nodded. At one table, a younger cowboy, flush with drink, was staring at his cards with a scowl on his face. Suddenly, he slammed them down. The slick-looking gambler in the black suit and a flat hat looked at him with a slight smile. "Somethin' wrong, boy?"

The youngster looked across the table. "I'll say. I think you been pulling cards from the bottom of the deck."

The gambler put his cards down on the table and put his hands out in front of him. "You calling me a cheat, boy?"

"Yeah, I'm calling you a cheat."

"You ready to back your mouth, son?"

The kid looked around, his face red and sweat running down, and then he reached for iron. Suddenly, his arm was in a grip of steel as was the outstretched hand of the gambler. Carson Budrow stood over the table, his hands holding the two men motionless. "I wouldn't do that, son. He's got a hold-out up his sleeve." Budrow squeezed the gambler's arm, and a derringer popped out of his sleeve. "You'd be bleeding out before you even touched that hawgleg of yours." He turned and looked at the gambler. "Now, if you don't want me to turn that deck over and show the kid if he's right, I'd take your stake and head east. Your call."

The gambler looked around, was going to say something, and then thought better of it. He started to scoop up the pot, but Budrow chuckled and held his hand tighter. "If you really think you won the pot, you can take it, but I'd suggest you pull your bet and beat it. Leave the pot for the boys to split. A gesture of reconciliation, shall we say?"

The gambler gave Budrow an evil look, pulled a few bills out of the pile, and left the table. The kid looked after him, then turned to Budrow.

"Thanks, mister. He would have bored me, sure. How'd you know he had a pistol?"

"Educated guess, son. Let me give you a word of advice. If you're going to drink, don't gamble. You're a little too skittish, looking on red likker seems to shut your common sense off."

Budrow turned and walked back to the bar and picked up his drink. As he stood next to Roads, one of the quiet, tough-looking men sidled up next to them.

"A pretty piece of work, stranger. That kid is gonna get himself shot one of these days. Thanks for helping him out."

Budrow finished his glass. "I just don't like to see someone that foolish buck a stacked deck."

"Well, that kid is the younger brother of a pretty big man around here. I'm sure he'd like to say thank you himself. You boys looking for work?"

Roads pulled out a cheroot, struck a match on the bar, and lit it. "Lookin' for my sister."

The man looked puzzled. "And who's your sister?"

"The *Chica Bandita*."

"You Granite Roads?"

"That's right, and I got some family business to take care of."

"Well, your sister rode through three days ago with a bunch of real hard cases, but she didn't look like she was expecting a family reunion."

"Any idea which way they headed?"

"Well, I heard 'em say something about Burnt Camp down by the Solitario."

Roads picked up the bottle and poured the man a drink.

"You sure you boys don't want to meet my boss? If you need a few days' work before you travel on, he could use some riders. We're right in the middle of a big drive, and we need some boys to help us keep the rustlers off."

Road looked at Budrow. "Kit?"

"Well, I could use getting my stake back up. I wouldn't mind if the pay is good."

"Good, fellas. Tell you what. Meet me at the hotel restaurant in the morning, and I'll take you out to the ranch. Jake's my name. Jake Rostick. See you then."

CHAPTER 9

MIDNIGHT AND NOON

There was a lot of lean, dry land and the cattle were scattered far and wide, looking for grass and shrubs. Sledge, the boss jack who worked for Mister Pentree and the Double Bar Cross, had offered a dollar a day and grub, but he wanted the spring roundup finished in a week. He had his own crew, of course. Nevertheless, at a dollar a day, he demanded Roads and Budrow pull the weight of four men.

Roads had found six head in a dried-out wash—heck, everything was dried out—and taken a break in a patch of shade beneath a big old boulder, sipping at his canteen, chewing at a strip of jerky. Most of the grub had been what he called field rations—beef jerky, biscuits like the rock-hard ones they'd gnawed on in the war, and dried apples. But a good map Sledge had drawn showed Roads and Budrow where the springs were, and fresh water was all a man needed. That and a good roll of tobacco and maybe a spot of medicinal brandy. The medicine he did not have, the tobacco he did. So, he took a while to enjoy a smoke, blowing it out into the dry heat that surrounded him.

Sometimes he worked with Budrow, Jake Rostick, or Cliff Briars, another one of the Double Bar Cross crew. But there was a lot of ground to cover, and a lot of beef to bring in, so most of the time everyone worked alone. Roads inhaled, held it, then blew out a long stream of white. He hadn't seen Budrow, or anyone else, for two days, possibly three. If someone had a wreck, they wouldn't know until it was too late to do anything about it. Never mind having bad luck with rustlers or Indians or a stampede. The risks were great, the pickin's slim, but that's the way this job was. There weren't too many ways to earn good, solid money in Texas with the war only a few years gone.

Yet, Roads admitted it rankled him. Every day earning a Yankee buck meant his sister was getting farther away, her killing spree unabated, robberies mounting, the Roads name dragged deeper into the muck. He thanked the good Lord the papers called her *Chica Bandita*. It was a popular moniker and sold their rags and lined their pockets. And it kept them from digging up dirt on her real name, her unmarried name. No one was interested in that right now, and he hoped it stayed that way. "I thank my Southern Baptist God for the small mercies," he said out loud, finishing his cigarette. "Because indeed the small mercies are often the great mercies."

The cattle were content to eat the bushes in the wash. They were not restive. Roads needed a siesta. Sharpsburg was out of the heat with his own boulder. Roads had a skin of water just for him, and there was plenty left. He'd give him another drink in half an hour. Pulling his hat down over his eyes, Roads tried to rest.

But there was Claret Black as soon as his eyes closed. He cursed. She had been tormenting him every night. Was she now going to invade his afternoons? She displayed a fine figure, a beautiful face, and long-shining hair. She was as strong as any two men. She filled him with desire. However, too much had already happened on this trail. There was no going back. He wanted nothing more to do with her.

"Talk to me, Granite," she urged.

"I won't," he responded.

"You want to."

"I don't."

"You do. I know you better than you think." She leaned over him, resting a hand on each of his knees. "It's been a good while since we kissed."

"And it will be a good while longer."

"It doesn't have to be."

"It does have to be. I can't think straight when you break into my thoughts like this."

"Poor boy." She laughed. "I really do have you over my saddle, don't I?"

"I swear, it wouldn't surprise me to find out you were casting some spell right now with Athena's help."

"Funny you should say that, Granite. She has dabbled in it. I don't know if I believe that mumbo jumbo. But she swears she can tell us where you are and the best spot to ambush you and Kit. Because that's what we're going to do. Jump you, punish you, and hogtie you both. Then we can be sure you won't get to your sister first and make her dance from a tall cottonwood. And this time, we'll hogtie you for good."

"Ridiculous."

She leaned farther over him till their lips almost met. "Sure you don't want a Texas kiss, Colonel?"

"No. No." He felt desperate.

She laughed. "You really are one hot mess now, aren't you? You know, when you first arrived, you were a corporal. Now you're a colonel. How did that come to pass?"

"I was always a colonel."

"So?"

"There were foolish demotions. Nonsensical reprimands. Now I've taken my proper rank back. Does Lee know? Jeb? Stonewall?"

"Jeb and Stonewall are dead." Her lips brushed his. "Let me back in."

The scent of her hair was intoxicating.

"No," Roads responded.

But his reply was weak, and she knew it.

She kissed him gently.

A fire coursed through his whole body.

She saw, smiled, and kissed him again. "Let me back into your life. You need me, Colonel. You were not meant to be a loner forever. You were not meant to be a bachelor. I am your bride."

"Claret, please."

"*Claret, please?*" She threw back her head. "You truly are mine. Give it up."

Roads leaped to his feet, shaking his head to get rid of the dream.

Sharpsburg snorted and stepped away.

The cattle ignored him and kept on feeding.

Roads rolled another cigarette, his hands trembling. He lit it, burning his fingers with the match.

"It's the war," he muttered angrily. "I know about this. I've seen this. Artillery barrages. Musket fire from a hundred thousand firearms. Men shot to pieces and dying all around your feet. You lose your mind. You see things. Hallucinate. And if Athena is spelling anything, she's planting Claret like a witch in my head. It's nonsense. I don't believe in witchcraft and hexes. I don't believe in magic. But I know war can rattle the brain. I guess it has come to me late."

Still smoking, he put the saddle back on Sharpsburg. "Sorry I startled you. Let's get well clear of here. Maybe we can leave the phantoms behind. Let's get the cattle to Sledge."

It was not a long ride, nor was it arduous. He did not have to get the cattle all the way back to the main ranch. Years ago, the brand had set up a large corral closer to the desert and the wilderness. It was a holding pen for roundups in the fall and spring. Cowhands—including two rough-and-ready cowgirls who worked as hard as the men and took sass off no one—only needed to bring the strays this far. Later on, other cowpokes would drive them to meet up with the main herd at the Double Bar Cross. It saved time and meant the ones rounding up the loose livestock could spend their time just on that.

Roads arrived well before sundown. He appreciated the extra daylight hours that came with spring. By the time he reached the corral, he had twenty-five head bearing the Double Bar Cross brand. The women came out to meet him, and the first words that came to mind when they drew close was "rugged splendor." These were the words he had used all week while rounding up cows and calves. Some might see the land as bleak. But he saw the power and the glory too. The raw magnificence. The "rugged splendor." And the two cowgirls.

Even in their saddles, he could see they were as tall as he was. They were in shirtsleeves and denim pants, so their strength and fine figures were obvious. As was their hardware—both wore a brace of Navy Sixes, modified for cartridges, a pistol on each hip. Ivory-handled. Which looked smart against their gun belts' black leather.

As for their faces, he could not say. They were both scarved against the dust the cattle kicked up in the corral. The bandanas were bright yellow and a deep red. Their hats were high quality, their long hair tied back, one raven, the other the color of harvest, their eyes a piercing blue. It was like getting hit by bullets when they looked him over.

"Thank you, sir," the raven told him. "We'll take over."

It was a woman's voice, but not a parlor and cognac voice.

The other tugged at her hat brim. "Much obliged, mister. Sledge invites you to stay the night and get some hot grub. You can head back out come sunrise. Says he needs to talk to ya too. If you be Colonel Roads CSA."

"I am," Roads responded. "But the CSA is over and done."

"Not to me it ain't," said Red Bandana.

"Nor to me," spoke up Yellow Scarf.

Roads smiled and shook his head. "True Texas spirit. I confess you both have the advantage over this CSA officer. I have no idea of your names."

"Our names are Midnight and Noon," explained raven. "You can guess why."

"Your faces are a mystery," he replied.

"And they can stay that way."

"You appear to be sisters."

The two women were silent a moment.

"Maybe," said the one with the harvest hair.

"I apologize for my lack of manners." Roads swept off his hat. "It's an honor to meet you both."

He was sure their eyes crinkled from hidden smiles.

"Thank you, kind sir," the dark-haired one said. "We appreciate chivalry."

"We do indeed," said the other. "There is precious little of it in this stretch of Texas, but it is always welcome."

"Forgive me, but this seems odd you are here and not in San Antonia de Bexar."

Again ... a silence. But they squared with him. Roads felt it before they spoke.

"We get paid in livestock if we do two more roundups after this," Midnight said. "Cows and calves and a breed bull. We want to start our own outfit."

"No men in on this venture?"

Noon snorted. "We don't need men. If we require any, all we have to do is whistle."

"I can imagine."

"Can you?" Noon's eyes crinkled.

"I am a Southern man, and you are Southern belles. I can indeed."

Noon coughed. "A long way from belles now, mister."

"I think not. Women like you are never a long way from belles."

"You don't even know us."

"High breeding is obvious. Even scarved, jeaned, and booted with spurs."

They both laughed.

"Charmer," said Noon. "Are you not?"

"The silver-tongued cavalier," Midnight added.

"At your service."

Without another word, the two women turned away, driving the twenty-five head before them to the corral. Roads decided it was best to leave them be and headed for a tent where he saw men lined up. He took care of his horse, making sure Sharpsburg had oats and water, tied her off, then joined the other cowboys, grabbing a tin plate and a spoon. The cook looked him over.

"Who are you, mister?" he asked.

"Roads."

"Colonel Roads?"

"I am, sir."

"Welcome. Double portions. That order comes from Sledge." He ladled beans and bacon onto Roads's plate till it was heavy. "Your buddy was in just the other day."

"What? Budrow?"

"Yeah, Budrow the Yankee. Gone back to the desert this morning. Pentree's oldest son with him. You met Lee?"

"Not yet."

Evening sunlight covered the camp. Roads sat off by himself and spooned the beans into his mouth. Just like war days. He thought about the two sisters, grateful they actually had the power to lift Claret from his thoughts and make him feel less haunted. He wondered who they really were and what was really up.

One thing was certain. They weren't Nettie, Claret, Annette, or Athena with rough ways and rough talk. Their language and their accents gave them away. Midnight and Noon were high born and high bred. They belonged in hooped skirts and coiffed hair, their fine hands holding red wine in crystal goblets. They ought to have been in Southern social circles in Richmond or Savannah. What were they doing here? He didn't buy their talk of starting their own outfit. Something else was going on.

Sledge found him. He was holding two tin cups of coffee, and he offered one to Roads. Then sat next to him while they drank and watched the sun dip down into the flatlands. After a bit, Sledge cleared his throat.

"You are doing good work, Roads. I wish you'd stay on. Mister Pentree would give you extra wages and a wrangler position. But I know you have it in you to bring your sister to justice. That's the word I got."

Roads said nothing.

"I wanted to warn you," Sledge went on. "Last couple of days, we've been getting reports about a band of Comanche kicking up dust hereabouts. I got twenty rifles or more in camp, but you and my outriders only got their pistols and a few Yellowboys. I want to make sure you go back out with plenty of ammo and extra grub, all right? Try to hook up with Budrow and Rostick and Lee. Cliff Briars too. You need to stick together for now till the Comanche move on. Ain't no tribe harder to deal with than the Comanche, Roads. They lick the Apache every time the two tribes clash. They're pushing their enemies west and taking their land from them month after month."

"Thank you, Sledge," Roads responded. "I'll keep my wits about me."

"I mentioned the same to your pal and to Lee too. I want you all to meet up at Red Rock Springs. Make that your camp. It's marked on the map I drew for you with an R. Plenty of water and grass there. Or what *we* call grass anyhow. The moment you get fifty or sixty head bring 'em on in. Don't none of you go after cattle alone anymore or drive 'em by yourself like you did today. It's too dangerous. You'll end up on the hard end of a Comanche knife."

"Yes, sir."

Sledge stood up. "'Nother thing. The two sisters. They're hard as flint. Don't mess with 'em. They're not interested. The black-haired, Midnight, she broke a man's arm just last week. She made it look easy. So, steer clear."

"I intend to. I have no romantic inclinations toward them."

"None, huh? Then you'd be the first. Even your buddy Budrow the Yankee looked twice."

Roads grunted. "They are women without faces. I am not stirred."

Sledge planted his hands on his hips. "They never unscarved?"

"No, sir."

Sledge grinned. "I'll be. Guess they like you and are going to pick their moment. God help you when they do. You're not likely to be such a monastic then."

"I shall endure, sir."

★★★

The next morning, it was just a silver cut of dawn when Roads woke. He ate some hot beans and coffee at the tent, filled his saddlebags with jerky and cartridges, and found Sharpsburg. He had barely saddled up and was on his way out of camp, one hand resting on the Yellowboy in the scabbard on his left, an extra pistol wedged under his gun belt, when riders loomed up on either side of him. He reached for the pistol, but a familiar voice called out.

"Go easy, my chevalier. If we'd wanted you dead, you'd have been eating dirt five minutes ago. Isn't that the quaint expression? Eating dirt? Hardly drawing room vocabulary. I wouldn't even have used a gun."

It was Midnight.

She was on his left. Noon on his right.

Both still scarved.

"What's this?" Roads demanded.

"We're heading out with you. Sledge thought it would be a good idea for you to have some extra guns along. Times being what they are, Colonel."

"He did, did he?"

"He did. It wasn't an order. Just a request. Noon and I decided to acquiesce."

Roads looked from one to the other. "Why? It's deadly out there."

Noon came up close, holding him with her eyes, eyes that turned to gold as the sun lifted free of the desert. She reached out and patted his knee. He felt that all the way through his body. Whether she was aware of his reaction, he could not tell. Her eyes remained a curious mixture of gold and blue colors and a look of raw steel.

"We are deadly too, Colonel Roads," she replied. "Very."

CHAPTER 10

WILLOWS AND CHOLLAS

Carson Budrow enjoyed the dirty work more than he let on. Since he had come west and hooked up with Roads, he had changed from a soft wealthy eastern boy into a western man. He wore his guns low and tied down, and after lots of practice, he had become fast and deadly with his Colts on both sides. Now scouring the range after wild cows that hid out up the canyons somehow seemed to fit the romantic dreams he had back on the banks of the Potomac—dreams of the west, wild Indians, vast herds of buffalo, mountains that scraped the sky and prairies that ran from Canada to the Mexican border.

Those had been the idle, halcyon days of a wealthy, irresponsible youth. He had been a wastrel, living off his family's wealth and shunning the more mundane demands of life such as learning how to make his own way. He had tried to ignore the disappointment on his father's face as he watched the direction his son was heading. It had been a great day when Budrow joined the army, although he had only done so to impress the lovely daughter of a rich banker. For some foolish reason, he thought he'd be home in a week, parading through town with a hero's welcome and rewarded by the lovely young damsel falling into his arms all atremble. But that's not how things turned out, and as he looked back, was a good thing.

Though his father had finagled a lieutenant's bars for him, he still had to go through training. Then Carson Budrow found out how unmanly he had become. It took some nasty taunting and a few harsh fistfights—which he came out on the wrong end of—to open his eyes to the sad state of his life. After that, he trained harder than anyone, working himself until he could feel his body harden under the harsh discipline and minimal diet. He found a fellow easterner from the tough streets of Philadelphia and befriended him. Jock Dennehy showed him the basics of boxing, wrestling, and some pure street fight moves he practiced daily. Once he learned them and was confident ten weeks of rugged physical work had given him an edge, he went back to the men who had beaten him and corrected the error of their ways with a few deadly left hooks to the wind and a couple of rock-hard right hands to the face. After that, they left him pretty much alone.

But it was the war itself that brought out the real man hidden inside him. Being responsible for men under his command and discovering a sense of honor and a long-hidden courage in the face of devastating enemy fire molded his character and changed the way his men looked at him. He went from a nose-in-the-air sissy boy to a man his men trusted ... and followed. The making of a man had come to a head in the barn outside Atlanta when he found three of his men preparing to rape Annette Devereaux. He could have laughed it off, turned, and walked away from what anyone would have considered a few good Union boys letting off some steam with a white trash southern woman. But when he saw the determination on her face, he knew the woman would kill as many "good Union boys" as she could and then throw herself on the tongs of her pitchfork before losing her honor. Something hitherto undiscovered in Carson Budrow's makeup rose in him, and he drew his pistol. When his men refused to stop and came at him, he did what any man of honor would do. He shot two of them dead and ran the other man off. Sadly, it didn't turn out well for him. The rat who got away went to an officer who had a grudge against Budrow. The long-time major had watched Budrow earn his captain's bars ahead of most of the promotions in their outfit, his included, so he ginned up some charges against Budrow and nearly got him hanged. A friendly jailer with an extra key had given Budrow the means to save his life but end his army career. Budrow shook his head and thought about everything that had happened since then. He didn't like that his family thought him a murdering deserter, but he had stood for what was right, and the entire episode opened the doors to his present life. So, it had all worked out well.

"That was a long time ago, Ranger ... lot of water under the bridge."

The black horse pulled his head to the side and snorted. His ears went up.

Instantly, Budrow came to full alert. He'd partnered with this horse long enough to know the big black heard and sensed things minutes before the man forking him suspected anything. Then he heard it, racing horses coming his way fast. Whipping out his colt, he stood up in the stirrups to see over the cholla bushes lining the trail. Roads! Coming on the run with Midnight and Noon hot on his heels.

Quickly Budrow jumped Ranger out onto the trail. Roads saw him and pulled up short, the two girls following suit.

"Good! I was hoping I'd run into you, Kit." He pointed back down the trail. "Comanche! Big bunch and hot on our tails. Raiding party, it looks like, and they will want these horses."

"And our scalps," the raven-haired woman spoke.

Budrow couldn't see her face, but her eyes were grinning.

"Where are the boys camped?"

Budrow wheeled Ranger. "We are down by a big buff wallow at the creek. Follow me." He touched his heels to Ranger and the big horse jumped out, running almost full speed before he had gone three steps.

Roads cracked the reins on Sharpsburg's neck and lit out behind him, the girls neck and neck.

An arrow whistled past Road's head as they cannoned down the trail.

★★★

Five minutes later, they raced into the camp, Budrow, Roads, Midnight, and Noon and the two pack horses tailing along. Jake Rostick was there with Cliff Briars. They both jumped up.

Budrow leaped off Ranger and dragged his Henry out of its scabbard. "Where's the Pentree boys?"

Rostick pointed through the trees. "Johnny and Lee went down to the creek to fetch some water." Budrow pulled his pistol and fired two shots. "That will bring them."

They heard a couple of shots in reply and then the heavy boom of a Spencer.

Roads had jumped off Sharpsburg and looked around, quickly sizing up the situation. "We are going to be in the middle of it in about five minutes. I say we hit into that wallow over there and push up the edges as best we can for a defensive wall. Grab every round you got."

Just then, Lee Pentree burst through the brush into the camp. "They shot Uncle Johnny. He's shot bad."

Budrow nodded. "Where is he?"

Lee pointed. "He crawled into the willow brake down by the creek. He's got his rifle and two pistols, so he can probably hold 'em for a while."

Roads pointed at the pack horses. "Lee, grab all the ammunition off those horses you can carry. You other boys grab the guns and head for that buff wallow on the run."

"What about the horses?"

Roads shook his head. "Cut them loose and head them off. Sharpsburg and Ranger had their fill of Comanche back at Horsehead Crossing, so there isn't a Reddy in the state that could catch them. We'll have to trust providence to save our scalps. Let's go."

The crew leaped into action. Budrow grabbed Roads's arm. "I'm going after Johnny."

Roads shook his head. "That's a long chance, Kit."

"Well, we know what the Comanche do to white men. You wouldn't leave me down there."

Roads grinned. "Seems like the Almighty has sent you to watch Johnny Pentree's back. Go get him then. And watch yourself."

The crew raced to the wallow, carrying as many guns and as much ammunition as they could hold. Budrow slipped away into the brush.

Then the Indians burst into view.

Cliff Briars looked them over from his position behind the wall of the wallow. "Comanche and Kiowa. Bad luck."

Roads took charge. "Let them get close, then let them have it. Keep up the firing until they back off."

The Indians saw them in the wallow and immediately charged their horses.

"Hold!" Roads shouted. The Indians closed within fifteen yards. "Now!" shouted Granite.

A solid wall of fire and lead vaulted from the buffalo wallow. The front rank of horses and riders tumbled head over heels right to the edge of their position. Another fusillade and the remaining riders turned and rode away.

Jake Rostick checked his loads. "They'll be back. Hold tight and stay low."

***

Down at the creek, Budrow was on his hands and knees, quietly making his way through the willow brake. "Johnny," he hissed, "you in here?" Nothing. He crawled a little further. "Johnny?"

Then he heard a sound behind him. Quick as a cat, he rolled over, just as a large brave, armed with a knife, leaped onto the spot he had just been laying. Budrow lifted his Henry and struck the brave full in the face. The man crumpled without a sound.

"Budrow, that you?" Johnny Pentree's voice sounded weak.

Budrow pushed through the willows. Pentree was lying up against some saplings, halfway sitting up. Both pistols were out and ready. A large stain of red covered his shirt front. Budrow crawled over.

"How are you doing?"

"Well, I don't think they hit the lung 'cause I ain't coughing blood, but I sure am bleeding like a stuck pig."

"Can you crawl?"

"I think so."

"Good. We'll head back toward camp. Follow me and stay close."

The two men begin to inch their way back toward camp. They heard a blast of rifle fire followed by another. The air was filled with the screams of the wounded and the sound of hooves pounding away.

Budrow looked back at Johnny. "Looks like the braves got a little more than they bargained for. Good thing Roads and the girls brought all the ammunition."

"The girls are here?"

"Yep, and a good thing for us they are."

They came out of the willow brake and slid underneath a tall cholla. The limbs were just high enough to keep them from being stabbed by the vicious thorns. About fifty feet away, they could see the tops of several rifles sticking out of the wallow.

Johnny stirred and moved closer. "Good thing that wallow was there. Makes a pretty good fort.

Just then, they heard drumming hooves, and the Indians came back for another go.

Budrow put his hand on Johnny's arm. "Wait until they get between us and the wallow and then shoot 'em out of the saddles. Aim high so we don't hit any of ours."

The Indians came thundering up and began circling the wallow and firing on a dead run. Budrow leveled his rifle, Johnny followed suit. When the Indians came around the backside, they rode right into Budrow and Pentree's field of fire.

"Now!" cried Budrow, and they cut loose. Three Indians went down and then two more. The crew in the wallow immediately deduced what was happening and concentrated fire where the Indians were thickest. A big warrior with an eagle headdress went tumbling face first off his horse. He tried to rise, but the report of a pistol rang out, and he flopped into the dust.

Budrow grinned. *Roads!*

Immediately, the other Indians tried to pick the big fellow up, but before they could get him on a horse, another withering blast cut four more of them down. The other Comanche rode away, howling and whooping.

"I don't think they'll be back," said Johnny. "That was Man Afraid of His Horse. Big chief. By the looks of him, he's now walking in the happy hunting grounds. The rest of them will go powwow and elect a new chief. Now would be the time to light a shuck."

Budrow and Johnny crawled out of the cholla bush and headed for the wallow. Jake Rostick was cussing at a bloody hole in his arm, and Cliff was nursing a wound above his knee. Lee's face was bloody, but he grinned. "One of them shot my hat off and took a piece of my scalp with it. That's about all the hair they'll get from us."

Roads and the girls were unhurt. Roads whistled, and in a few minutes, Sharpsburg and Ranger came running up, followed by several of the horses.

Roads looked down at Johnny. "How are you, Pentree?"

"Well, if you can get me back to the ranch, Cookie is a mighty good doctor, and I might make it."

Roads looked at Budrow. "What did I tell you about the Almighty?" he turned to the rest. "Saddle up quick. We got maybe an hour before they settle their election and come back, although I think they will probably head home, licking their wounds."

CHAPTER 11

COMANCHE SCARS

"Mr. Roads, sir. Colonel."

Roads had seen the two women coming toward him, though the campfire was out, and the sky was black, starless, and moonless because of clouds. Midnight and Noon. Unscarved. Which he hadn't noticed during the short, sharp fracas with the Comanche. Ordinarily, he would not have missed it. He had suspected their beauty simply from their eyes and eyebrows, the only things showing above their scarves as they had trotted their mounts beside his to meet up with the others.

They were both astonishing in their looks in different ways. Something, no doubt, the other women had not appreciated when they'd seen the two with their scarves down. He was surprised Athena had not caught up with them and shot them in the back during the melee with the Comanche. It certainly was not something he'd put past her.

He had a hard time understanding the game Athena was playing and what she wanted out of it. Money, certainly, but what else? A reputation as a desperado? Her own gang? Power? That she desired romance, he doubted very much.

She'd as soon shoot a man or gut him with her butcher knife she swore was from the Alamo as kiss him on the lips.

Roads swept off his butternut CSA slouch hat. "Ladies. It's good to finally see you both as God intended."

But it was not a Savannah mansion's parlor or drawing room, and neither of the ladies—the one raven-haired, the other blonde as sunlight—were inclined to flirtations with a Southern man, however handsome and charming.

"Mr. Roads," Midnight continued. "Do you have much experience fighting Comanche or Apache?"

"I do, as it happens," he replied. "You saw me fight, didn't you? I grew up in Texas, and their raids are not uncommon. Sometimes they come in waves of six hundred or more and sweep down to the Gulf, killing and torturing and burning for hundreds of miles, wiping out the smaller settlements. There is little that can be done to stop an attack of that size."

"But you have resisted them."

"I have. My whole family has."

"Including the sister of yours I am told you are tracking."

"Indeed. She is a soldier in her own right."

"Then why do you want to kill her?" Noon demanded.

Roads shook his head. "I do not wish to kill her. But she has slain others in cold blood many times now, including her husband, who was a rogue and vagabond but not a man without redeeming features, and certainly not deserving of the bullets from her gun."

Both the women squatted by him. He caught a whiff of perfume, expensive, and was a bit startled since neither Claret nor Nettie would take such bottles on the trail with them. Though he knew Annette would and probably Valentina Cooper and her younger sister Betsy.

Valentina Cooper. My, my.

Valentina was a woman of twenty, almost twenty-one now, and though raised in a rough-hewn way, on a hard scrabble farm, by a tough-skinned mother, he knew she wanted to be a lady one day with all the lace and frills. Betsy wanted to be like her sister. They alone carried the rich scent of Midnight and Noon on their skin and clothing.

Valentina's blue eyes shimmered like something priceless melted down and poured. He knew he was having a hard time resisting her attentions. Maybe he'd stop trying. Her beauty equaled or surpassed Claret's and so did her shooting skills and her spunk. He supposed he was ripe for the plucking since Claret had bushwhacked and buffaloed him—he had no further interest in her, amorous or otherwise. The door was shut and locked against Claret Black, and there were no glass windows. For all he knew, he would fall to Midnight's or Noon's considerable charms.

He wondered what Budrow thought about Nettie. Had things changed drastically for him too since she'd trussed him up like a prize New England turkey and pistol whipped him into compliance with her plans? Such humiliations were not easily forgotten or forgiven, especially when delivered by a woman upon a man.

"Colonel?"

"Mm?" He had been distracted. "How are you two faring?"

"We are all right."

"Are you considering matrimony on this journey?" Roads teased.

"Matrimony? What brought that up?" She laughed softly, aware the others were sleeping, and wiped the back of her hand across her mouth. "Not likely. But it's been my experience plans can change rapidly."

Roads nodded. "So it is in war."

She smiled. "So it is in love."

"We didn't come here to talk about love," Midnight spoke up. "Who else in the group has experience fighting Comanche?"

"Why, Nettie and Claret are Texas gals. They know what to do. You'd have seen that if you'd watched the pair of them fight like Budrow and I have."

"What about the Coopers?"

"The mother will kill anyone and anything as if they were no more than a tick. Hesitation or conscience do not abide in her. The three girls are handy enough and don't hold back. The boys are no help."

"What about your particular friend?"

Roads snorted. "Budrow? The dang Yankee? He acquitted himself well enough. As did our other men."

Midnight thought about this for a moment. "None of them are as tough as the women."

"When it comes to frontier women, no, men rarely are. They rely too much on their bravado."

"Even drawing room women. With knives in their boots and derringers in their bosom."

Roads saluted. "I grant you that."

"We heard they turned you two inside out." He saw Midnight and Noon smirking in the darkness. "Hardly what we'd expect from Indian fighters—being caught flatfooted by two Texas belles. They could have killed you both if they'd been of their minds."

"I agree. They were trusted. Now there is no more trust."

"Yet you rode with them easily enough," Noon pointed out.

"That was then, this is now."

"What are your intentions?" she pressed.

"My intentions are my own."

Noon gave Roads a poisonous look with narrowed eyes. "Not if you all are riding with me, they aren't. What are your plans?"

Why he felt he should explain himself to them, he did not know. "I will ride with the others until the day comes I must strike out after my sister on my own."

Noon patted his knee. Roads felt that. Which he knew she knew. "We figured. We'll be with you."

"Why? Do you want the money?"

"Not at all. We'd like to form a gang with her."

"What?"

"Her headlines are inspiring. She's a free woman. Does whatever she darn well pleases. We both want to be part of that."

Midnight was still smirking. "You'll do whatever we tell you to do, sir. You'll take us to her and leave the others out of it. There's two of us, one of you. You have to sleep. Either of us can gut you like a catfish and probably enjoy it more than Mrs. Cooper. But, of course, we don't want to do that. We need you alive. At least until we find your Alice. Then we won't need you at all. It'll be up to her to decide what to do with her long-lost brother, who is so easily duped by a pretty smile and a splash of French cologne. We'll take your guns. All of them."

Noon extended an open hand.

Roads grunted. "This is getting to be a familiar theme."

"Just give me your pistols and knives."

"I'm not inclined to give those over to a woman a second time."

"I don't have time for your bruised and foolish manhood."

Roads didn't see it coming. Noon drew back and struck him on the jaw with her gloved fist. He fell back, stunned.

Midnight delivered the second blow, crashing into the side of his head with a hard kick from her boot. With Roads out cold, they went through his pockets and took away everything they wanted, not just weapons—his cigars appealed to them as well. His rifle was nearby, and Noon put it on her own horse. Then they dragged him farther away from the group, gagged him, and slapped his face till he came to.

Midnight smiled into his eyes. "How do you feel, Colonel? Looks like your cavalry has been bested again."

Noon smoothed back his hair. "I think we both know more about the Comanche than any of you. There's a good reason." She tugged down the collar of her shirt and showed him the dark angry markings tattooed into her flesh. Along with the scars, long, white, and vivid even in the darkness. "There's more, but I'm not undressing for you. I think you get the point, Colonel. If you think flint is hard, think again. I can crush flint in my hands like penny candy."

"Here is what you don't understand, Mister Bourbon," Midnight spoke up. "We know this Comanche band. You think they won't be back? They intend to put us afoot. An attack didn't work out well, so now they'll resort to stealth. They won't send in many. Probably only two or three to steal our horses. We won't hear a thing. But we're going to be right there with our mounts. And these Comanche won't hear a thing, either."

"You'll help us kill them," added Noon. "Knives will be sufficient. We'll give you back your Bowie. But please understand. If you try anything, we'll carve you up and find Alice on our own. We're excellent trackers. If you shout out for the others, we'll cut them down as they come running. We won't even blink. So, shut up and do what you're told. Nod if you comprehend."

Roads nodded.

Noon patted his head. "Good boy. Here's your Bowie." She put it in his hand. "I'm taking out your gag now. Be quiet as a mouse. Red Swan will be here."

She removed the gag, and Roads gasped, thankful for the air.

Midnight let him see her small but wide blade—a blade meant for skinning. "You think it will be Red Swan?" she asked her companion.

"I spotted him in the raid. Moon Child too."

"Then leave Moon Child to me."

"Of course. I have Red Swan. The colonel can have whoever is left."

"What if there's only two?"

"He can watch." Noon grinned. "Maybe he'll learn something about fighting from us."

Midnight flashed her skinning blade again for Roads's benefit. "Just remember, sir. You know what kind of women we are now and who made us into stone killers. Compared to what I've been through, taking your soul with one cut would be easy."

Noon wriggled forward on the ground. "Now, we crawl."

They kept Roads between them. Midnight was at his back. He had no intention of trying anything other than killing the Comanche who were after their horses. The women's eyes may have sparkled when they wanted them to, but behind that sparkle was the flat black of death. This was not the time to deal with them.

The horses didn't knicker at their approach, just remained standing motionless, tethered to a long rope tied between boulders. By Roads's count, the three of them waited an hour. Then, without hearing a thing, he spotted a Comanche untying Budrow's horse. He had barely noticed him before Midnight had taken the man from behind and slit his throat, using the skinning blade she had taunted Roads with. A few horses down, another brave untied Roads's mount, Sharpsburg. Noon pounced before the knot was loose in the Comanche's hands. She had a longer blade, similar to Roads's Bowie.

She flipped the warrior onto his back, plunged her knife into his stomach, then ripped the thick blade upwards to his jaw. As he gasped and died, blood spraying Noon, she reached in and yanked out his intestines, hurling them to the side, spitting in his face, and saying something in Comanche, biting out her words. Roads saw no more than that, for he glimpsed a third man coming up on Noon. He ran at her. She lifted her knife against him, but Roads dived over her body and took the Comanche at the knees with a loud cracking sound.

Just like in war, there was no time for thinking things through. Roads choked the Comanche with one hand and drove his Bowie into the man's heart with the other. He had never seen a man die so quickly. In a heartbeat, the Comanche stopped moving and lay as motionless as a heap of rocks. Roads's breath was coming hard and fast.

A hand rubbed him up and down his back. It was Noon. She smiled into his face.

"You'll do, Colonel," she said in a quiet voice, continuing to rub his back. "Your muscles are all knotted up. I can help with that." She rubbed harder, digging her fingers in till he almost cried out with the rough pain. "We may ask you to join our outlaw band. I'm sure your sister would like that. I believe I might too. All you need to do between now and then is keep your mouth shut."

CHAPTER 12

BLACK SUN, BLOODY MOON

Carson Budrow walked up to the chuck wagon. "Anybody seen Roads?"

Lee Pentree shook his head. "Not since last night, Budrow. He was talking with Noon and Midnight, kinda quiet like, by the fire. Just as I climbed into my bedroll, I seen 'em get up and head toward the remuda."

The first edge of dawn was just peeking over the eastern hills. Budrow nodded to Lee. "Let's go see what's up."

They headed out to where the crew corralled the horses. As they approached, a coyote slunk away from something lying on the ground. Budrow pulled his colt and waving Lee back, walked quietly forward. A Comanche brave lay on the ground, dead, a very surprised look on his face. Someone had separated him from his bowels with a very sharp knife, and that probably accounted for the look. Two more bodies lay in grotesque positions further down the mesquite fence. Budrow motioned to Lee.

"Where did these Comanch come from, Budrow?"

Budrow shook his head. "Looks like someone interrupted them as they were trying to set us afoot. Go get the crew, Lee. There's something fishy going on here."

While Lee hightailed it back to the camp, Budrow walked around the corral, gun drawn. Ranger cut himself out of the herd and shuffled up, looking for the treat Budrow often carried.

Budrow rubbed the horse's forehead and looked around. *Sharpsburg is gone!*

He ducked under the fence and pushed through the herd. They were nervous, suspicious, and the ears of most of them were up and flicking around.

Midnight and Noon's mounts are gone too.

Just then, Jake Rostick hurried up. Cliff and Lee were right behind.

"What's goin' on, Kit?"

"Did you see Midnight or Noon back in the camp?"

Jake scratched his chin. "Come to think of it, no. I thought they were down at the crick washin' up."

Budrow holstered his gun. "Some Comanch got in here last night. They were probably trying to set us afoot so the rest of the band could cut us off. They didn't get the job done." He pointed at the three bodies. Two of them were cut up in a grisly fashion, the third was stabbed in the heart. "I reckon the ladies did the cutting on those two. I've never known Roads to go beyond what was necessary. And Sharpsburg is gone, along with the ladies' horses."

"What do ya think it means, Kit?"

Budrow looked around. Out of the corner of his eye, he caught the flutter of something white up against the fence. He picked it up. It was the wanted poster Roads always carried.

Chica Bandita!

"I think those women have either convinced Roads to take them after Alice, or they took him at gunpoint. And I think it is the latter. Or he wouldn't have dropped this."

Budrow walked around to the gate. Sure enough, the tracks of three horses marked the dirt. "Jake, I'd say they left just after dark. Who was watching last night?"

Cliff spit a wad. "Me and Jake. Swear we didn't hear anything, Kit."

Budrow looked down at the tracks. "That's because they put moccasins on the horses' hooves so they wouldn't ring on a stone. Those girls are pretty sharp. How long have they been trailing with you?"

Cliff spit again. "Only about a month. They rode in here from over east. Showed us right away what they could do with a rope and a rifle. Couple of tough ones. Seemed awful sweet, though."

Budrow scowled, thinking of Nettie. "It's the sweet ones that will hog tie you."

"What are you gonna do, Kit?"

"Well, I wouldn't leave Johnny down in the willow brakes with those Comanche on his tail, and I won't leave Roads in the hands of women who appear to be nastier than the Comanche. Jake, if you could give me what Roads and I have earned, I'll be tailing out after them."

Lee stepped forward. "Do you need someone to go with you?"

Budrow shook his head. "I appreciate your offer, son, but it looks to me with Johnny down and just the three of you to ride the herd, you'll be needed here more."

Cliff nodded. "That's for sartin. What with them Comanche around, we need to get these cows back to the ranch."

Jake pulled his wallet. "I reckon you boys earned top hand pay, so here's two hundred each. Obliged for all your help. Lee, give him an extra rifle and as much ammunition as he can put in his bags."

"That's real decent of you, Jake. I'm glad I scraped acquaintance with you back in that bar. You boys have been good to work with. I'll see you when I see you."

Budrow walked back to camp, fetched his saddle and his gear, and within twenty minutes was riding out.

The crew watched him go. Cliff bit another chaw off his plug. "There goes the real deal."

★★★

Granite Roads rode between the two girls. They sat easy in the saddle, but he knew they were watching for a move—any move—on his part.

Roads, I hope this will teach you there's no woman can be trusted.

Midnight laughed. "You know, Noon, I bet he's thinking back over the last few months and deciding there ain't one trustworthy gal on the face of this planet."

Roads jerked his head around. "What, are you reading my thoughts now?"

"Nope. It was easy telling what you were thinking. You look like a dog who just dropped a big hambone in the river."

Roads pulled a cheroot out of his pocket. "And here I thought all women were sweet little gals that would do their man's bidding without complaint."

"You mean their master's bidding, don't you?"

Noon pushed her horse alongside Sharpsburg. "You know, Roads, you're a fairly agreeable man, when you do what you're told."

Roads lit his smoke, took a long drag, and then blew it in her face. She jerked back.

"Tell you what, lady. What I learned in the war is that the tide of battle can turn in a split second. I wouldn't be counting any chickens just yet."

"Just like all those riverboat tinhorns, aren't you, Roads? All talk and no action. Only one thing on their mind ..."

ZIIINNNNG!

The bullet hit a rock close to Granite's head and went careening into the distance. A fusillade followed the first shot, along with some Comanche war whoops.

The three riders didn't hesitate. Spurring their horses into action, they headed for a narrow wash just ahead. Just as they started to go in, the heads of three Comanche showed over the lip.

"Not in there!" Roads shouted. "They got us boxed." He spurred Sharpsburg. "Follow me! I'll need a gun!"

They turned back toward their attackers, and Noon tossed Roads her Henry as they headed straight toward the Indians coming at them. Roads levered the Henry and shot the two leading bucks out of their saddles. The other five jerked their horses' reins in confusion, and Roads led the two women straight through their ranks. Midnight and Noon had their pistols out, and each one shot a brave through the body as they rode by. They were headed away at a full gallop when a rifle barked. Noon's horse went down, throwing the girl right over its head. Noon twisted like a cat in the air, landed on her shoulder, and rolled. She sprang up. The speed of their charge had carried Midnight and Roads at least a hundred feet past where the horse went down.

"Roads!"

Without hesitating, Roads pulled Sharpsburg to the left, and the big horse spun almost completely around. Roads headed back. The girl was up and running with the Comanche coming on hard.

"Noon! Swing up!" Roads swung low to one side of the racing horse with his arm out. Noon ran into the circle and swung gracefully onto the back of the big dun. Roads pulled Sharpsburg around and headed back the way he had come. Bullets ripped by them as they rode hell-for-leather toward a rocky outcrop. They leaped off, dragged the two horses behind an outcropping of rock, and dropped behind some boulders. They could hear the Indians howling their rage and disappointment. Roads pushed the horses further back into the protection of the rock walls and grabbed ammunition out of his bags. He ran back to the girls, who were flat down behind the rocks, looking for targets.

"I'll need my Colts!" Roads thundered.

"In my saddlebags!" Midnight yelled.

Roads raced back, got his guns, then hustled back to their position. The Indians were riding hard across the opening, trying to ricochet shots off the walls. Noon fired her pistol and a brave shrieked and pitched face-first into the dirt not twenty feet away.

Roads thrust the Henry out and picked off another rider. Immediately, the Comanche turned and rode back the way they had come. Silence settled over the scene. It had grown dark. Roads looked up. Dark clouds were forming overhead. A few drops of rain spattered on the surrounding rocks, evaporating quickly on their sun-warmed surface.

Roads checked his loads. "Looks like we're in for some weather. The Comanche will probably sit out the storm, but when it passes, they'll be back."

***

Budrow had followed the trail of the three horses about ten miles when he saw another set of tracks cut the trail of the three riders. The horses were unshod.

Comanche!

Budrow slipped his Winchester out of its scabbard and rode cautiously ahead. He counted twelve in the party that was trailing Roads and the women.

If there's twelve behind, they probably sent some ahead to bushwhack them. They'll need some help.

He pushed Ranger into a lope. The big black picked the trail right up and forged ahead. After about an hour, Budrow pulled Ranger up and listened. Nothing. The air had turned colder. Ahead on the horizon, a low mass of black clouds was forming. Budrow saw a bolt of lightning flare out, then a few seconds later the low rumble of thunder. Ranger's ears flicked forward, and he snorted nervously.

"Looks like we're in for a gullywhumper, boy. We better find some shelter."

Budrow had been riding down a narrow canyon with steep sides. The gray and red cliffs rose above him, and the sun was disappearing behind the black clouds. More rumblings and another flash. Budrow looked about. The walls rose steeply with no breaks. He pushed on. Away off in the distance, he thought he heard a rifle shot, a volley and then some more shots, but it was hard to tell because of the thunder. A few drops of rain fell and suddenly it was coming down in torrents. A towering bank of clouds swept out of the western sky—tossed in the heavens like the crashing wild waves along some fog-bound, rock-strewn coast. The front of the mass was dead black and blood red, with gray in between, a bulging, mushrooming, vast monster devouring everything before it. All of heaven's breath pushed and piled the clouds until they were roiling in an ungovernable mass of destruction.

A bright explosion in the storm's heart burned out like cannon fire, flashed from the west to east, and died. Then from the depths of the deepest black burst an explosion of sound. It was like mighty cannons firing in a deafening volley along the crags and parapets of the clouds, and the crushing sound seemed to roll on and on and then fall down upon Budrow with malice and vengeance. Another flash rent the darkness, and the rain blew sideways before the howling wind.

Budrow looked desperately around. There! In the flash from the lightning, a hollow in the cliff face. Budrow pushed Ranger forward, and in a minute, they were under the rock wall out of the main part of the storm. Budrow looked around. By the light from the flares, he could see the back of the hollow opened into the dark. A cave.

He led Ranger forward, and then he struck a match and peered into the darkness. Someone else had used this place for shelter because there was a pile of Juniper and a fire ring. Breathing a sigh of relief, Budrow got a fire going and then he pulled the saddle off Ranger and rubbed him down with the blanket. He looked in his bags. Stuffed in behind the ammunition was a bag with some dried meat and another bag with some grain.

Lee, bless his heart.

After graining Ranger, Budrow ate some of the meat, set his clothes to dry, and settled down to wait out the storm.

★★★

Morning came and Budrow awoke. Ranger nickered, and he poured some water into his hand from his canteen and moistened the horse's mouth. He went to the mouth of the cave. The storm had passed, and the first faint light of dawn lit the sky. He saddled up Ranger and led him out. The moon was still up, hanging low in the sky over the canyon wall. It was blood red and full. Budrow pushed Ranger ahead down the canyon. After about an hour, he saw buzzards circling. Pulling up, he dismounted and quietly led Ranger forward.

There was a turn in the canyon, and he carefully looked around before he stepped out. Over against the wall on the other side lay the body of a horse. Someone had stripped it of its saddle and tack. Budrow came slowly up. The rain had washed out most of the sign, but he could still see tracks leading toward a rocky outcropping. He approached cautiously. Behind the rocks, he saw several spent shells, then some tracks in the wet sand. Two horses with riders. One of the horse's hooves sank deeper into the sand than the other.

"Ridin' double."

Superimposed over the tracks were the imprint of moccasined feet.

Budrow looked at Ranger. The horse was munching some dry grass beside a rock.

"Whoever was here is gone, Ranger. Looks like the girls are riding one horse and Roads the other. They must have lit out while the Comanche hunkered down out of the storm. Then the braves showed up after they left."

Budrow followed the tracks down to a creek bed not far away. Torrents of water had washed all the sand away, leaving only bare rock. The tracks disappeared.

Budrow took off his hat and scratched his head. "If Granite is hiding his trail, those Indians will be hard put to catch him." He patted Ranger's neck. "They headed down this canyon, so that means somewhere along this creek bed, Roads probably doubled back and went out another way. And it will be an act of providence for me to find them."

CHAPTER 13

FAYE MEADOWS

Once the storm swept past, Midnight found what Roads felt was a tolerable den of rocks in something of a circle that would afford them decent protection from another Comanche attack. There was a cleft they could place the horses in to prevent their theft. Midnight also made sure they returned all his weapons to him.

"If we get out of this alive," she told him, "just do what you want, Colonel. Go back, go ahead, it doesn't matter to me and Faye. Only let us do what we want to do."

"And what is that?" Roads checked over his weapons. "You still want to join my sister?"

"We do. Are we going to have to shoot you over that?"

"No. Do as you wish. But I don't understand why you want to turn outlaw."

"We want to be free of laws men make that favor themselves and do women wrong. We don't want towns and cities run by your gender. We want to be free of all that. Entirely free. This is the best way."

"Fair enough. I can either ride ahead or behind, but I am going for my sister as well."

"To kill her? We can't let you do that."

"I will not kill her."

"Then what will you do?"

"Take her alive."

"What if she doesn't want that?"

"I shall be persuasive."

Midnight laughed. "Still think you're quite the Southern charmer, don't you?" She traced a finger gloved in deerskin down his face. "Well, maybe you are. But charming a lady is one thing. Charming a sister who's turned *desperado* is something else. I guess we'll wait till the day arrives. You'll have to cut through her men."

"I accept that."

"We won't help you with it, but we won't get in your way, either. That's your play. We'd much rather have an all-female gang, so you'd be doing us a favor."

"No back shooting?"

Midnight's eyes hardened to obsidian. "We've never done that, and we're sure not going to start with you. We'll kill you face-to-face."

"Much obliged." He smiled. "You two have water and ammunition?"

"Plenty."

Roads settled in. He saw where Midnight nested herself but could not spot Noon. He took note that Midnight rubbed sand and grit over her rifle barrel to make sure the sun did not glance off the metal. She'd make a good soldier. And a good outlaw. She'd ambush many a stage and many a gold shipment. Just like his sister, men and the newspapers would fall in love with her dark beauty and dangerous ways and glorify her. It was the way of the world. Why did such things entice?

The three of them waited, sweating it out in the heat of the day, but the attack Roads expected did not take place. Darkness came fast when it came and some welcome coolness with it. He continued to watch and wait, sipping from his canteen now that the sun could not pull the moisture out of him through his skin. Noon suddenly appeared and surprised him. She had made no sound and was crouched by his right arm.

"You should be an army scout," he told her.

"Robbery pays better."

"But remains dangerous."

"So is soldiering."

"You move about like a feather, Faye."

"She let it slip, did she? Well, tit for tat then. Her name's Sindy with an S."

"Faye and Sindy. The two beauties."

"The two bandits."

"Hm. Both titles have their charms."

Faye stood up, tossed her hat, shook her long blonde hair loose, and undid her gun belt. She let the belt with its two holsters and pistols drop on his stomach. He *ooofed* and cussed, and she laughed, towering over him in her boots. "I thought you were a tough hombre." Then she swept the gun belt aside and lay down with him. "You saved my life," she said.

Her lips were on his before he could open his mouth and reply. At first, it was in his mind to resist. But he felt the strength in her kiss, and in her fingers, fingers that removed his hat and ran through his hair, tugging and pulling as her passion mounted, and he let go. He gripped her like she was life and death.

"Comanche," he managed to get out.

"Shut up," she ordered. "I'm in charge, and I'll tell you when it's time for talking. Sin can handle them. Besides, we know this bunch just like we knew the other bunch.

They won't attack at night unless they can get at the horses. And to do that, they'd have to come right over us. They know what Sindy and I can do with a knife. They taught us. Like most men, of whatever race, strong women who fight back frighten and intimidate them. So, let's get back to our little romance here. Desert nights are bitter. Warm me up, Roads."

Faye pinned Roads firmly to the spot, pressing him into smooth rock and sand. "I've seen the way you look at me. You've been at that since we met. Do you think a woman doesn't notice the secret glances? I guess we pick up on them a lot more than men think. So, I know this is what you want, Colonel. Now I want it too."

"I thought men were no good. Just low-down stinking coyotes."

She laughed and kissed him on the forehead and on his tangle of hair. "Cute and clever. But there are always exceptions to every rule. And you are Faye Meadows's exception."

She overwhelmed him—her kisses rich and deep and fierce. Roads surrendered to the happiness she brought him. He'd had little enough in his life.

Her scent was as beautiful and essential to her spirit as her lips. Leather, sweat, horse, burnt gunpowder, steel, dust, and some kind of sweet cologne she must have splashed on. Her strength and intensity were irresistible.

"Got you in my rope now, Colonel," she teased. "What are you going to do about it?"

"I will simply enjoy it. The war was long and dirty. You are preferable to armies, muskets, and bayonets. This trail itself has been arduous. And my name is Garrett."

"Mm. Nice name. Strong name. What about the other women in your band?"

"There is nothing to say about them. The season is over with Miss Black, brief as it was."

"Are you sure? She's radiant."

"I'm sure you're the woman to define radiant."

"Am I? Imagine. How gallant of you. *Una chica mala como yo*. A bad girl like me, as rough as a farrier's rasp, has captured a corner of your heart, Garrett."

She reached into his shirt pocket and plucked out one of his cheroots and a box of matches, giving him a final long kiss on the mouth. "It wasn't even that hard. I wonder what would happen if I tried harder?"

Faye rolled over on her back, smiling at her thoughts about romancing Garrett Roads, and struck a match against her boot heel, shielding the flame with her hand. She blew out a stream of smoke, sighing with contentment. "It might be we could have a good life together, Garrett."

"The Comanche will smell that tobacco."

"You worry too much, *mi gran hombre*. Can I call you that? Never mind. I will anyway. White Owl knows we're here. His whole band knows we're here. Whether I smoke or we do the romance matters not one little bit, sir." She leaned over and inserted the cheroot between his lips. "Let me help you relax. Breathe in."

"Faye ..."

"Shh. Obey my commands, and life will go much easier for you, *mi gran hombre*. You'll see."

He inhaled. Held it. Yes, of course, it felt good. Then he exhaled, and that felt good too. She let him have a few more puffs and then put the cheroot back in her own mouth, kissing him as she did so.

"Which is better?" she asked.

"You," he replied.

"You're learning." She handed him the matches. "Join me."

He fished out a cheroot, lit it, and waved the match till it went out.

Faye planted one of her boots on his and raked his leg firmly and purposefully with her spur. "*No te gustaría ser su gran hombre malo hmm? No es así como te gustaría ser conocido?*" She rolled onto her shoulder to face him, smoke curling from her mouth and nostrils. "Wouldn't you like to be my big, bad man? *Si*? Isn't that how you'd like to be known? As my big, bad bandit? *Mi hombre bandido*?"

"What are you asking?"

"In a way, I'm telling. You can't kill your sister. We'll drill you and plant you in dirt before we let that happen. You can't take her, either. Try and we'll stretch you from the nearest cottonwood. So, you're staying with us. Or you're leaving us for good. But if you do, you won't have me, Garrett. And I'm kind of a nice person to have around, don't you think?"

Faye finished her cheroot and stubbed it out against his hand, watching to see if she could make him flinch. He was aware of her game, bit down on his cigar, and did not move. She grinned. "Ah, mi gran hombre *duro*."

She snuggled up against him. "Aren't the stars beautiful? Think about what I've said, mi hombre. Sleep on it. Sin is good with my plan."

"What about my sister and her men?"

"Her men? No, there won't be any men. If you don't kill them, Sin and I will."

"An all-woman gang with one man?"

"*Sí*, an all-woman gang with one good, bad man."

"And my sister?"

"Why, your sibling is your problem, Colonel. If she wants you dead, you're dead. Nothing we can do about that. If she wants you to ride with us, all your family issues are solved. It would be a helluva life with me. So free. So wild. So romantic. Don't disappoint me, Garrett."

He felt the cold barrel of one of her pistols press into his shirt and ribs.

"I lied, you know," she whispered. "You can't ever leave. You're stuck with me and Sindy till you corpse. We can't have you leading a posse back to us, can we? I know you're the kind of bulldog that won't release his bite. So, this is your shotgun wedding, handsome. You're going to ride with us. No going back. If you have any ideas about using us to get to your sister and then disappearing, think again. We already figured on you trying. Double cross us and we'll Comanche you. You know what I mean, don't you? Nod for me. Good boy. We have amazing knife skills Black Crow taught us. Sin and I can keep you alive for hours while we skin you. Hours and hours and your screams won't bother us none. Don't double cross us."

"I have no plans to do that."

"Good boy. You're drawn to me, Garrett, like a moth to the fire. I'm warm and pretty, but I'll burn you alive too. The truth of it is, you need Faye Meadows and the danger I bring into your life. I know you miss the war and everything about it, sir—the action, the excitement, the gunfire, cannon explosions, cavalry charges, sabers, the killing, the smell of blood, a smell like copper and iron. I'm the one who can bring all that back to you and give you a life worth living again. You won't be happy tied to apron strings, Garrett. But I guarantee you'll get the excitement you need to thrive strapped to my gun belt."

"You make a convincing case, Miss Meadows. You missed your calling. You should have been a lawyer."

"Oh, I haven't missed a thing, Colonel. I'm my own lawyer, judge, and jury. I'm making my own laws from now on. You might say, I'm a law unto myself. And you're going to love having that kind of life with me."

CHAPTER 14

A LONG AND WINDING TRAIL

Budrow climbed off Ranger. He was down in a small canyon away from the sun. In front of him was one of the *tanques* common throughout desert regions—a depression worn in the stone by wind and sand that filled with fresh water after every storm. This one was big. It stretched back and around the corner of the draw. There was nothing growing beside it because nature etched it in solid granite. He bent down and dipped out a handful of water. It was sweet.

He pulled Ranger's head down. "Must have come from the rainstorm, old boy. It's good. Drink your flll."

Budrow had been looking to pick up Granite's tracks since the morning after the big storm. While he was making a wide sweep trying to cut the trail, he stumbled on the *tanque*. Budrow walked up a rise above the hollow and looked around. He was high on the side of a pass through the mountains that crossed Big Bend country. Off to the west, across a barren, windswept stretch of sage desert, and far off in the haze of dusk, he could see another range of mountains with a spectacular edifice gleaming in the dying sun.

"That must be the Guadeloupe Mountains, Ranger. El Paso is in that general direction."

The place where he stood was on a little knoll with a sweeping view of the country ahead and behind. As he strained his eyes, he thought he saw something far off in the distance.

A small cloud of dust, about a day's travel ahead. Must be Roads.

He continued his sweep. There! A bigger cloud, farther to the south and behind the first sighting.

"Looks like the Comanche are still on the trail, Ranger. But they are way back too. Granite must have really hidden his trail. I'm just lucky we got up so high, or I never would have seen him."

He turned away when his eye caught another plume. This one was far to the west. He had only seen it because it was bigger than the other two and the sun had glinted off something shiny in the middle of it.

Alice and The Ten! Or Athena! Whoowee, looks like we're all headed for the same place.

Budrow shook his head. Ranger looked up at the motion. Budrow frowned. "This reminds me of the day I stood with Buford outside Gettysburg and watched Dick Ewell bringing his whole division up the Cashtown Road, Ranger. We're in for a scrap, for sure."

Night was coming swiftly, so Budrow made camp at the water hole to get some rest. He collected some dry mesquite from a thicket at the mouth of the small draw, then built a smokeless fire. After graining Ranger, he warmed some biscuits and dried beef on the heated stones and boiled a little coffee.

The sun was going down in a fiery ball in the far west. Orange radiance flamed a huddle of high clouds. Behind them, the deep indigo of night filtered up from pale blues and golds. Across the way, a coyote began a song. Then the desert night came quickly.

Budrow thought about Nettie. He realized he missed her. Her warm arms, her soft lips, her bravery and nobility. He remembered the night he had pulled a Kiowa arrow out of her smooth white shoulder, shortly after they met. She had opened her blouse fully and grinned at his discomfit at seeing her naked bosom.

"What's the matter, Budrow? Ain't you never seen one of those?"

He smiled at the memory. Annette Devereaux seemed to pale in comparison.

"This whole deal with Alice has sure boogered everything up, Ranger."

The horse nickered in response.

★★★

The sun came like it had set—orange fire peeking over the hills to the east, then a golden halo as some drifting clouds caught the first rays. Budrow was already up drinking coffee. He finished the cup, pitched the last drops with the grinds into the morning fire and then picked up his gun belt from where it lay beside his bedroll. He strapped it on and tied both guns down. He loved his old Navies, but they were still a little clumsy for a fast draw.

Colt needs to make something a little more balanced.

He stood still for a moment, hands at his waist. Then quicker than most eyes could follow, the pistol was in his hand. He tried it again, and again, making sure his hand got warm and stretched. Then he drew with his left hand, a trick he had picked up from Granite. He was only slightly slower from that side.

When he felt he was up to a gunfight, he grained the horse, ate some dried beef, and hit the trail.

★★★

A day's ride ahead, Granite, Faye, and Sindy were following a dry stream bed through a winding canyon. Faye and Sindy were riding double, and Roads was in the lead. The canyon walls disappeared for hundreds of feet, and there was no sand beneath the horses' feet, a bad sign.

Roads turned around in his saddle and spoke to the girls. "The rock on the floor of this canyon is polished smooth because when it rains, this place probably fills up ten feet deep and a lot of water comes through here real fast. That's why there is no sand. Sure hope we don't get another one of those gullywhumpers like we had the other night."

Sindy grinned from behind Faye. "I should smile, Roads. Let's pick up the pace."

Roads urged Sharpsburg into a trot. The iron on his hooves struck sparks from the granite streambed and rang like church bells in the confined space between the red canyon walls. The girls continued to ride behind. Blue skies visible in the cleft above them were turning into a somber gray. From time to time, they passed side canyons, some of them barren and dry and some with piles of debris jammed into corners.

"If it rains, there will be a wall of water coming down every one of these tributaries," Roads shouted back. "Keep moving, or we'll be swimming to New Mexico."

Up ahead, Roads could see the canyon widening. He urged Sharpsburg to a canter. More light came into the narrow crevasse, and sparse vegetation began showing along the edges of the bed. A slight turn and they were out into a wide place in the canyon. Beyond a confusion of boulders, a slope led down into the brown, sage-covered desert, a wasted landscape that disappeared miles ahead into a gray haze.

WHAM!

A bullet ricocheted off a rock to Granite's left.

WHAM! WHAM!! Two more shots came in a rapid tattoo.

Granite jerked Sharpsburg's head around and headed back toward the canyon on the run, the girls right behind him. When they got back into the chute, Roads leaped off his horse and dragged Sharpsburg behind the rocks lining the entrance to the canyon. The girls slid off their horse and sent him after Granite's bay.

"Shoot fire and go naked. What have we run into now?" Granite spit and peeked around the rocks.

WHAM! Another rifle shot pinged off the rock tight beside Granite's face and went clanging up the canyon. Granite wiped his face, and it came away bloody.

Faye ducked down beside Granite. "That's not Comanche, Granite. I only know about three warriors can shoot like that. That's white men."

Granite hunkered down behind the rock and pulled the girls down beside him. Above them, the skies were roiling with nasty-looking storm clouds. "That's either Athena or some of The Ten. We're in a fix here. We can't go back because we'll be in the middle of that chute when the water comes pouring down. A death trap, for sure."

Faye put her hand on his arm. She was looking up at the wall. "How about if I go back to the last side canyon and get up the wall? I can get above them, and we'll catch them in a cross-fire."

Roads looked at Faye. "Sounds like a fool idea to me. Those walls were steep."

Sindy grinned. "We used to call my sister the Lizard when we were kids. I've never seen a wall she can't get up. She takes her boots off and up she goes. Guaranteed, she'll be up there before the storm hits."

Roads looked back and forth between the girls. "Okay, I'll take your word for it. Can you make an owl hoot?"

Faye nodded. "Didn't live with the Comanche for nothing."

"Okay. When you get up, give us a hoot so we know you are up. Then, if you can see where they lay. Put some rifle shots down and we'll go at them from here."

Just then, a voice called out. "Roads? Is that you, Roads?"

"Who wants to know?"

"We come bearing word from your sister, Alice."

Roads leaned against the rock and pulled out a cheroot. He nodded to Faye, who slipped up the canyon headed for the side draw. "Ah, mi chicá bandida. And what does little sister have to say for herself?"

"She says she's tired of you trailin' her. In fact, she's pretty much plumb wore out and is about to lose her patience and her sisterly love. And, to top it off, she's about to write you off as a brother."

"She wrote me off when she killed Joby and my nephew."

"Aaahh, Roads, you don't know the entire story. It's not fair to judge without hearin' both sides. Why, Alice is just as innocent as a newborn lamb." Some loud guffaws followed the remark. Roads peeked around the rock.

"All I know is Joby and Jimmy are worm food in a hasty grave back on the Roads Ranch."

"Why … didn't you hear, Roads? Joby lost the ranch to Todd in a poker game. It's the Yancey Ranch now."

"The hell you say."

Granite looked around again. He just about had the speaker spotted.

"Yessir, Granite, that's the truth. If I'm lyin', I'm dyin'. Joby got into a big stakes game with the Bishop boys and Ferrell Kincaid and came up short, drawin' to an inside straight."

A low hoot drifted down from above. Granite looked over at Sindy, who glanced up and nodded.

"She's up," she whispered.

Roads looked around the rock again and slid his rifle out slowly.

Two quick shots rang out from above and Roads fired right after at the spots he saw the bullets hit. Above his head, Sindy's rifle answered. From across the swale, Granite heard a curse in Spanish.

"*Madre Mia!*"

The first speaker roared. "Roads, you polecat. Just when we was having a right friendly palaver."

"That you, Pitch? Sounds like you got Mateo there too."

"Dang right, and you're going to regret those bullets, Roads."

"Gee, Pitch. I'm sharing the trail with a couple of compadres, but I don't speak for them. I don't think they took too kindly to the bullets you greeted us with when we came down the canyon."

Sindy yelled out. "That's right, you varmint. I don't like to dance with a desert rat I don't even know." She whispered to Roads. "Give me cover." More shots came from above, and Granite added his rifle to the fusillade. Sindy dashed across the mouth of the draw to the other side and dropped behind a boulder. Now the trio had a wider field of fire. They poured fire into the boulders.

The outlaws across the way responded in kind. Lead was flying like angry bees. Just then, Granite heard something that chilled him. From behind the outlaws came a chilling war-whoop. Comanche! Gunfire erupted behind the outlaw's stronghold.

"Looks like we got company, girls."

Just then, a jagged bolt of lightning split the dark sky. Thunder shook the surrounding ground. Roads yelled at Sindy. "Call Faye down. It's going to get mighty uncomfortable in a minute."

Sindy gave a peculiar whoop and yelled, "Faye."

Within a minute, Faye was beside them, pulling on her boots. The rain poured down. Roads grabbed the girls. "In a few minutes, the canyon is going to flood. Our friends are busy at the moment, so follow me."

He led them on a run to the side canyon. There was a pile of driftwood jammed up against a corner. "Grab a stout log, big enough to float you and drag them down here. Strap your guns on your backs. When the flood comes, grab your log and ride it like a bronc. The flood will carry us right down that slope."

Thunder boomed again. Rain poured from the sky.

"What about the horses?"

"Sharpsburg will follow me. The other horse should follow him."

Just then, they heard a strange noise, a low rumble, and a roar.

"That's the water coming out of the side canyons," Roads shouted. "It will be here in a minute."

The roar increased, sounding like a herd of buffalo thundering across the plains. Then, around a corner in the canyon came a wall of water five-feet high. A few logs and some brush roiled on the front of the wave.

"Horse!" Granite yelled. Sharpsburg's ears went up, and he took off at a dead run down the slope, the other horse close behind.

"Grab on, ladies! We are going for a ride!"

The wall of water smashed down.

CHAPTER 15

OUTLAW GIRLS

Roads could never recount how they all swam out of it. A couple of times, he was sure he was dead and had fallen into darkness. When he gasped for air and stared with a wild desperation around him, he couldn't spot any heads. But as the surge dropped away, Sharpsburg somehow found a purchase, screaming and clambering, and hauled them both out of danger, clicking and snapping with her hooves. Roads collapsed on his stomach, spitting and coughing and choking. When he pushed himself up, two well-worn boot toes filled his eyes, dry as desert bones. He heard a lever on a Henry rifle slide and click, metal on metal.

Roads looked up into Athena's broad smile, her handsome rugged face, high-noon blue eyes and raven-wing hair. What was she doing here? Was he hallucinating? But no, it was her. No other woman wore her pants and shirt that way. She bragged it accentuated her finer qualities.

One hand kept the rifle pointed at Roads. The other lit a match by scraping it against her boot heel. Then she applied it to a fat and loosely rolled cigar clenched in her grin.

"Might as well make my play now, Roads, whaddya think?" she giggled with a strange sound in her throat.

"What are you talking about?" He felt too waterlogged to speak. "And what the heck are you doing here?"

"Why, the Lord's blessing on my life, we heard the fracas and came to see what was up. The gunfire, water, thunder, and such. Lucky for you we did." Athena blew out a stream of smoke as if, Roads thought, she was a locomotive. Roads looked around him. "Oh, Faye and Sindy are okay. My girls roped them out. Their horses are gone." She puffed on her cigar. "My thought was to shoot you instead of watching you drown. Seemed the Christian thing to do. But somehow that horse of yours hauled you up."

"No roping out?"

"No roping out. What the heck, I say. I'm gonna kill you, anyway. Hands, knife, hang ya, drill ya, any will do well. I admit I do favor the personal touch of a knife or hands around a man's throat. That is the big mule kicks to me. That is the thrill."

Roads saw Sindy vomiting up water. So was Faye, her blonde hair a mess of dirt and grit. Athena's daughters were coiling their lassos. Betsy was the younger version of her big sister Valentina, and Valentina was the younger version of her rough and tumble mother Athena. Both were dark featured, sky-eyed, and remarkably attractive. It was Stella—Shotgun Stella—who broke the mold with her straw hair and gap-tooth grin and eyes of emerald. She was the scamp, and proved Roads right in his assessment, when she mocked Sindy and Faye. "You ain't so good looking now, are ya? It's like you been partying all night, and now, you're losing your insides in the morning."

And there were Nettie and Claret and Annette. Their beauty and strength as startling to a man as ever. But their wrists were roped, and Athena's sons had pistols on them. Coop was arguing with his younger brother Seth, but their guns never wavered. Like their mother, the boys were wild, dark, and unpredictable.

"I say the silver-blonde will be my wife," Seth was declaring in his pipsqueak voice. He meant Claret.

"You're too young for a full-grown woman," Coop snapped back. "As for me, I'm going Mormon and aim to have all three for my wives."

"Ma won't let ya."

"Of course. she will. She knows I'll breed her the finest children and grandchildren. She's chomping at the bit for the outlaw gang she's so fierce for, ain't she? I'll help build it up solid."

Roads looked back at Athena. She still had her gun barrel on him, steady as a rock, grinning, smoking, and savoring his helplessness at her hands.

"Why are they tied?" Roads asked Athena.

"I have plans for them they ain't cottoned to yet. In time, they'll come around to my way of thinking."

"What is your way of thinking?"

"I want an outlaw band of my own more than I crave food and drink. They'll wise up to the advantages of being part of such."

He tried to take that in. His mind was still in a spin. Roads saw water and waves and Sharspburg fighting to get them free. The taste of the dirty water was raw in his throat. He finally climbed to his feet. Athena backed up.

"Don't try anything, Roads," she warned, "or you'll die sooner rather than later. And, like I said, I don't need a gun to do it. My fists have broken men's bones and cracked skulls like walnuts. Or there's my bull whip tied to my saddle. That'll cut you up just fine."

"What are your intentions?" Roads demanded.

"I kept you alive so I could tell you my plans and gloat. Lord knows I like to outwit a man and make sure he knows it. At first, I was gonna just gun your sister down and bring her body in for the reward. But blasting those desperados who bushwhacked you changed things. Don't look so surprised. We caught 'em from behind—there were three of them. Coop stitched one with three pistol shots, Stella shotgunned the other, laughing her fool head off while she done it, wild cat that she is. And I took my pleasure with the third, gutting him like a trout with my Bowie. See the vultures on them?"

Roads had noticed the big circling birds. "I see them."

"Coop reckons that's four of The Ten gone. He says they shot another up aways back. That's four of them dead and planted. Easy to kill, as most men are for a rough-shingled woman. So, I'm thinking now, the better route is to join your sister's gang and plunder the earth. Enjoy high times. Kill off the men by back shooting them during robberies and blaming it on law dogs. Then shoot Alice after a while and take over. Talking with Midnight and Noon weeks ago got me thinking that way. They'll come along with me and the kids. So will your belles, Nettie and Annette and Claret, your sugars. But you get planted here. Not that we'll bother to bury you. But this is where you'll stay till the vultures and wolves tear you up."

"Claret and Nettie and Annette won't go along with this."

Athena laughed, rolling her cigar about in her wide-lipped mouth. "You're such a fool. You think you're at some fancy Southern ball? Of course, they will. I reckon I'll keep them at gun point for now. But after they see how good an all-ladies gang can be, I'm sure they'll be more than willing."

"There are still men out there."

"I told ya. Easy to deal with. We'll cut 'em down. Just like we did these here others."

Coop and Seth prodded Nettie, Annette, and Claret over with their pistols. Roads's sugars, Athena had sneered. Faye and Sindy had guns on them too.

"Glad you both survived," Roads told Faye.

"We lost our rifles," she replied. "Sorry you won't be joining us, handsome. But an all-girl gang has its restrictions."

Roads caught Sindy's eye, and she shrugged, her Navy Six steady on Nettie.

"This to your liking?" Roads asked a gray and grim Claret.

She wouldn't look his way. "Nothing on this trail has been to my liking."

"Are you going along with it?"

"I have little choice, do I? Stop speaking to me, you miserable coyote."

Stella, the straw-blonde, laughed. She swung her shotgun on Roads. "She's right. Shut up, or I'll saw you in two." She grinned, the gap between her front teeth prominent. "You can still marry me. I prefer your partner something fierce. But I'll take you and pack you along in my saddle bags ... ha-ha. Soften up your bones with a few choice blows and stuff you right in."

Roads did not reply.

"It'll save your life, mister. And I ain't half-bad, you know."

"Where's the others?" Athena interrupted.

"This is all there was, mama," Valentina told her.

"Horses?"

"Yes'm, we got Sindy's and Faye's."

"God's will. You and Stella and Bets bring along Handsome's horse and gear. Toy with him if you've a mind, then shoot him when you're ready. It's a lot of fun, girls, killing grown men. I enjoyed it early on. Shapes you. The rest of us—Coop, Seth, the Sugars—mount up. We've wasted enough time. Sin and Faye, you both scout. Did you get the guns and blades off the Sugars?" She pronounced it Sugahs.

"Yes, ma'am," Sin responded.

"I'll bring up the rear. Let's get along. Kill anyone you see, Indian or white. We got no friends within a good hundred miles."

She tugged her hat brim and tapped cigar ash at Roads. "It could've been better. You might have shared my life. But we've butted heads since the beginning."

Athena and her sons rode away with the five women. Claret glanced back at Roads, and Athena smacked her with her Henry's barrel. "Stop gawking. He'll be in hell before you can count to a hundred and eight."

The moment Athena and her band were out of sight, Valentina swung her rifle butt into her sister's head with all the muscle she could muster. Stella dropped like a hatful of stones. Betsy and Valentina lashed Stella across her saddle, pinned a note to her back and swatted the horse's flank. The animal trotted off after the others, Stella bouncing up and down on her stomach.

"My Lord!" Roads exclaimed. "What makes you two think your momma won't come after you?"

He was frankly stunned, rooted to the spot. The trail had been a Texas twister from the start, and he'd been bushwhacked by the fairer sex more times than he could keep track of. He told Betsy and Valentina that. They both roared with deep laughs that bellied up from their stomachs.

"You're thinkin' we're the fairer sex, ain't ya? Whoever calls us that must be a mighty naïve man." Betsy was still laughing. "Is that how you see us, sir? You ought to reconsider. Me and Val call ourselves the rougher, tougher sex. Rougher and tougher and grittier than any town or city dude, that's for certain."

"After all this mayhem, week after week, I'm inclined to agree," Roads replied. "I'll never think of a woman as a flower again."

Valentina smirked, a perfectly wicked look crawling over her face. "Oh, we can be flowers, sir. But the kind with sharp, hurting thorns."

"So then, roses."

"That's right. Beautiful, lush, sweet-smelling, and hurting roses. We so enjoy it when men underestimate us. Typically, they don't figure it out till they're flat on their backs and full o' holes like a colander."

"And you think your mother with all her thousands of sharp thorns won't come after you for double crossing her?"

Valentina shook her head. "She won't, sir. She's smarter than any man, and she knows I can outshoot her and whip her to a lump of butter in a fistfight. Why, sir, just the other day I bested her three arm wrestles in a row."

"What did you write on the note?"

"*I'll kill ya, Ma.*"

"That's it?"

"That's more than enough."

"What if your sister Stella rides back?"

"Bets and I would convince her to throw in with us. But Ma won't let her ride back. And the truth is Stella ain't nothing like me and Betsy. She's the joker in the deck. But if you'd seen her put paid to that outlaw, you'd know she was a rock and stone killer too."

"Because she used a shotgun?"

"Is that what Ma told ya? Stella emptied four barrels into that poor hombre, two of them while he was begging for his life. Then she used a knife."

"To get a scalp," Betsy interrupted.

"She did a lot more carving than she needed to lift his scalp."

Roads was surprised and perplexed. "You knock out your sister and you'd gun down your mother. I took you for a close-knit family."

"Thick as thieves. And this is what thieves do."

"What do you want from me?"

"Nothing. Just lead the way, Colonel Roads, and we'll follow. But I can tell you this, sir. We need to get well ahead of them. Ma intends to knock your sister down. I don't care what folderol she filled your head with. Consider the source of her river of words. Y'all want a chance to reason with your sibling? You have to be there first. Chica Bandida and her Ten? Ma'll chew them up and spit them into the dirt like scrapings of grease."

Valentina suddenly swung up with her rifle and let off two shots into the blue. She laughed at the look on Roads's face. "Y'all afraid of me? If I'd wanted to double cross ya, you'd a'been long dead by now. That was just to confuse Ma. She's gonna wonder hard if I didn't blast the pair of ya. Let her chew on it. Meantime, we've got to go. Your weapons should be on your belt or saddle unless the flood took them."

The flood had indeed taken Roads's rifle and both pistols. He cussed. Valentina shushed him and gave him one of her Smith and Wessons. He immediately recognized it as a Model 3—a top break revolver that fired cartridges. He tugged on his hat brim. "I'm obliged to you, miss. This one's a dandy." It was shiny with pearl grips and a good long barrel. He reckoned six and one-half inches. She smiled because he looked like a boy admiring his first gun.

"It was a gift from a lover," she explained. "I had to shoot him a few months after. But you never mind that. I'm not my sister Stella. I'm someone safe to fall in love with despite what happened to poor lamebrain Arthur. Just shoot straight when the time comes, sir. My guts tell me we'll be fighting Ma's gang and your sister's gang both. Lord knows how we'll come out of it all." Valentina crammed her hand into a tight jeans pocket and came up with a handful of .44 cartridges, which she called Smith and Wesson American, and gave them to Roads. "And call me Val."

Roads took the cartridges with a nod. "Very well. If you stop calling me sir. I'm Garrett." Roads lifted himself into a saddle that was still dripping wet. "My idea is to try and cut the trail the outlaws used when they ambushed us. No doubt Noon and Midnight are doing the same. We'll go in a different direction and get well ahead of them and then loop back for the trail."

"Are we gonna ambush 'em?"

Roads gave Val a sharp look. "Not unless we have to." He set off at a trot. "We are on some kind of odd pony ride. One minute, our situation is this and another it's that."

"And what do you think of me, Garrett?"

"I think you're beautiful and charming, to be honest."

"What else?"

"I think you're strong and sharp as an Alamo Bowie."

"I like that. Your stock is going up rapidly. What else?"

"I think," Roads responded with a flicker of a smile, "that I have a tiger by the tail."

Val laughed deep and dark, throwing her glossy black hair in a fetching way. "Or she's got you." She reached over and put her hand on his arm while her sister smiled, Roads thought, in a rather extravagant and knowing way—*my sister's been here before.* "Don't fear me, Garrett. I'm the best lover you could ever have. No one finer. I know my way around a man. Let me prove it to you."

That night, after a soft, soothing time with Roads, Betsy asleep, and their campfire low with just a trickle of flames, Valentina put a bullet into Budrow when he came quietly upon them in the dark.

CHAPTER 16

PERDITION'S DOOR

Two days and nights of tracking left Budrow tired and worn out, and now this. He stood on the little knoll and looked down at the gory scene. Below him, scalped and bloated in the scorching sun, three bodies lay where they died, in what appeared to be an ambush spot above the mouth of a small canyon. Someone had come on them while they waited and brutally murdered them. Down below where the bodies lay, the swollen remains of two dead horses, legs twisted, and bodies jammed up in a pile of debris against the base of the rise. One was a horse either Midnight or Noon had been riding the last time he saw them. Budrow didn't recognize the other one, but it wasn't Sharpsburg. So, Roads might still be alive. Debris, mud, and driftwood littered the swale at the mouth of the canyon, and he could see the path of a flash flood going down the hill toward the playa below.

Budrow could picture the scene in his mind—Granite leading the two girls and working his way down the canyon during the gullywhumper storm, the three owlhoots lying in wait across the clearing from the canyon mouth, the wall of water coming down before they could spring their trap, and Roads and the girls swimming out, while two of their horses drowned in the flood.

But who had killed the bushwhackers? He climbed back on Ranger and rode slowly down the hill. He stopped and dismounted by the dead men and rolled one over on his face. They had shot the dead man from behind. Then someone cut them up. One man had deep gashes on his arms and faces where he tried to defend himself.

"He was still alive when they cut him up. Who would do such a thing, Ranger?"

Then it came to him. *The Coopers!*

He led Ranger to some brush, tied him, and scouted around. Sure enough, off to the side were the tracks of several horses standing in a group.

Athena, the boys, her three girls, and Annette, Claret and … Nettie. Quite a group.

Boot tracks marked the muddy ground. He went a little further. There was Sharpsburg's distinctive track, the shoes narrowing at the back, and he spotted where someone had been sitting on the ground.

That would be Roads. So, he's alive! But if Athena has her way, he might not be for long.

The tracks of the primary group of riders led off toward the west. Then Budrow saw something that puzzled him. Eight riders had ridden away. Then another set of single tracks followed them, but slowly, not running. Three riders remained, one of them Roads.

What the devil?

Then the three riders rode off in somewhat of the same direction, but not hard on the first group's trail.

Now here's a genuine mystery. Athena goes off with seven other riders. Roads stays behind with three. One of the three rides off alone. Then Roads and the other two head in the same general direction, but they are obviously not going to join up with Athena's gang.

Budrow shook his head. He took Ranger's reins and stepped up into the saddle.

We'll follow Roads. Maybe he can sort this out for me when we catch up.

Budrow kicked Ranger into a canter and headed off after the three riders.

★★★

Betsy, Valentina, and Roads sat around a small fire built in the bottom of a draw out of sight from anyone riding up. They had just finished some antelope meat they had fried on the hot stones. Dry mesquite wood fed the fire and produced little smoke. Around noon, they had cut the trail of the three bushwhackers Alice had sent. Athena's gang had obviously cut the trail too because the tracks they had been following took off back-trailing those of the three dead outlaws.

Valentina scowled.

"Ma's got the jump on us, for sure. We got to ride and ride hard to get ahead of them. There are only three of us, so we can go faster. We also have to trust our luck and see if we can outguess Ma." She looked up. The tracks headed off to the northwest. "What do you think, Roads?"

Garret lit a cheroot. "Mount Ord is behind us. Fort Stockton is off east. Only thing ahead is El Paso, and beyond that, the Cimarron of east New Mexico. We held some stock there when Budrow and I rode with Charlie Goodnight."

Betsy looked at Roads. "You was on that drive?"

Garrett nodded. "Yes, ma'am. We faced down Comanche at Horsehead Bend, tracked through twisters, floods, and wicked men. That's where we started ridin' with Nettie and Claret. Annette Devereaux showed up in the middle of the drive. I think she was a western gal just waitin' to be born again. Grew up all soft and pasty on the plantation in Georgia but rode horses all her life, and her daddy taught her to shoot the eye out of a hummingbird. Took her a while to acclimate. She got kidnapped twice, but she took a hankerin' to a .50 caliber pistol and helped me and Budrow take down Skin Ricketts and his gang. Shot three of them trying to get behind me while I was facing down ol' Skin. You girls think you're mean hombres, but I'm givin' you a lookout. Nettie, Claret, and Annette are three tough women, and if your ma relaxes her grip one minute, they will eat her up. And your brothers—braggin' about who's gonna marry and breed those gals. Nettie might forget that slight when hell freezes over. "

"So you think they will go to El Paso?"

Roads shook his head. "The Ten are down to four. We already got two outside Longhorn and those four dead hombres back there cut down the firepower a darn sight. So, they will skirt El Paso and the Rangers waiting for them there, I believe they will head for New Mexico. The people in the Cimarron are less interested in who's buyin' the drinks. I say we head straight for New Mexico and see if we can cut Alice's trail somewhere up ahead of your ma. I'm guessing they will stay east of El Paso and avoid the worst part of the Chihuahuan Desert. Gets mighty dry out there."

★★★

They rode hard the rest of the day. At sundown, they stopped to camp.

Valentina smirked at Roads. "You're welcome to share my bedroll, Garret."

Swift as a striking rattler, Betsy's colt was out of her holster.

"If he shares anybody's bedroll, it will be mine."

Roads grinned. "Now, ladies, you wouldn't be so mean as to make me choose between you, both of you bein' so lovely and all. How about if we hold off the romancin' until we can get to a tub with some hot water and soap? I reckon I smell somewhere between a drowned cougar and a rotten cactus."

The girls looked at each other. Betsy slowly slipped her gun home. "Wal, I reckon you're right. I'm not so appealing right now, either, and Val smells worse than me. But we'll have to sort it out sometime."

Valentina smirked again. "We can always shoot it out, Bets. If you don't already have the drop on me, you know I can put three bullets in you before you get the smoke wagon level to the ground. Haw haw!"

Roads busied himself starting a fire while the two sisters glared at each other. "You two can sort it out later. Meanwhile, we need some dry wood. I mean *really* dry, for this fire. We don't want any smoke tippin' off your ma as to our whereabouts. And since your ma didn't seem to bother teaching y'all to cook while she was showing you how to filet a man, I'll get some supper going."

The girls grumbled but went off on their chore. Roads went to Sharpsburg and pulled his saddle off. After brushing him down with some mesquite leaves, he opened his saddlebags and pulled out some more dried antelope meat and his camp coffee pot. Soon he had the meat sizzlin' on some hot rocks and the coffee boiling.

The two girls wandered back into camp, each with a generous load of dried mesquite.

Roads grinned. "That'll do nicely, ladies. Now sit and eat."

The girls set to eat hungrily, and soon the deer meat was a thing of the past.

Val pulled out her Bowie and picked a few flecks of meat from between her teeth. "You'd make somebody a good wife, Roads." Both the girls guffawed.

Roads shook his head.

Val smiled. "By the way, me and Bets worked it out whilst we was out grubbin' wood. You're mine tonight. And won't mind the smell."

Betsy nodded. "And mine tomorrow."

★★★

Budrow had followed the three all day. He had to push Ranger to keep up. Now, it was graying down into night. Way off in the distance, he had watched the cloud of dust marking Athena's crew, but he had seen little of Road's group.

Garrett's got them riding hard but quiet. Guess he doesn't want Athena to know where he's going. This sure is a puzzle.

His thoughts wandered a bit, so he didn't see the edge of the little wash and his boot slipped off the edge. He went down hard. As he stood up, he saw a red flower in the dark. Then again.

That's odd. The sun's gone down. I shouldn't be able to see ...

Something hit him low down in the side, something that felt like a mule kick and then another hit him high in the left shoulder.

I've been shot ...

And then his thoughts fled away.

★★★

Roads came running. Val was crouched over someone lying on the ground.

"He came up sudden like, Roads. I didn't know …"

Roads pulled a match and struck it. *Budrow!*

His friend was lying at an awkward angle, blood pouring from two wounds.

He jerked Val to her feet. "That's my friend, you fool." Before he could stop, his fist shot forward like a lightning bolt and caught Valentina on the point of the jaw. She went down like a shot buffalo. Betsy looked at Roads, her face stricken.

"She didn't mean it, Garrett, I know she didn't."

Roads snarled. "I don't give a hoot what she meant. If my friend dies, so do both of you."

Betsy's hand went for her gun, but Roads was faster. The Colt went flying off into the dark and Betsy's Bowie was jerked out of its sheath, and the razor-sharp blade was pressed against her white neck.

"You hell-bent Coopers think you are riding me? I've been going easy on you because we are headed in the same direction, and no real man cottons to shooting women. But you have never seen me angry. You are about to get an awakening." He pulled Betsy closer. "Can you nurse?"

Betsy nodded, her face white. "I've patched my kin some."

Roads jerked her over to the place where her gun lay, still pressing the Bowie against her neck. He picked up her gun. "Drop your belt."

She complied. He jammed the Colt behind his belt. "Now you help me get Kit into camp."

"What about Val?"

Garrett laughed. "She'll be seeing stars until the sun hits midday. Strip her weapons off and leave her where she lies. And don't get any ideas. Right now, I'd just as soon kill both of you as look at you."

Betsy took Val's guns and her knife, then followed Roads as he dragged Budrow back by the fire. All the Cooper bravado had disappeared, and she stayed meekly by his side.

Garret fetched out a blanket and laid it out by the fire. He put Budrow down and nodded at Betsy. "Get to work."

She stripped off Budrow's shirt. The wound in his shoulder was bleeding hard, but it wasn't pumping. Roads rolled him part way over. The exit wound was clean. The one in his side was the bad one, but it, too, had gone through.

"That one tore him up. We have to get the bleeding stopped and hope it didn't tear up his guts. Septic poisoning could set in."

He stood up and pulled a canteen off the tree branch where it was hanging. "Wash him up and tie up these wounds. Doesn't look like we'll be going anywhere for a while. And remember, I'm not happy with you girls, and my trigger finger is mighty itchy."

He walked out of camp to where Valentina lay. He looked down.

Thought you could get me with your feminine wiles! We'll see now, won't we, girl?

He dragged her limp body back to camp and trussed her up with a rope. Then he went to where Betsy was working on Budrow.

She looked up. "I don't know, Garrett. He's shot bad. I'm doin' what I can, but he might not make it."

Roads smiled a grim smile. "If he doesn't, neither will you." He jerked his head toward Valentina. "And neither will she."

142

CHAPTER 17

BAD BLOOD

Once he'd cooled, it did not sit easy with Roads that he'd been rough with a woman. Especially with Valentina. After all, he could not deny he'd allowed a few sparks to flicker in his heart for her. He shook his head. He shouldn't have let there be sparks to begin with.

Over the past few months, nothing good had come of his relations with any of the ladies on the ride. But rough and tumble as she was, Val intrigued him with her hard-edged beauty and her hard-living savvy. He didn't doubt she might turn the tables on him with a grin, toothpick in her mouth, eyes flashing as she drew down on him and made Roads her prisoner. He'd still want her. Yet all those thoughts were inconsequential now. She was in the doghouse and would remain there until Budrow pulled through.

Valentina apologized repeatedly. Roads allowed there was a sweetness and a sincerity to them. But she'd pulled the trigger on his wrath. Budrow might be a no-good Yankee, but he was Roads's no-good Yankee. Roads felt personally responsible for him. As he regained his footing, he acknowledged Budrow might just as well have been a bushwhacker. They had plenty of enemies out there—

Athena and her wild-eyed sons, four desperadoes, Noon and Midnight—and the Lord only knew what Nettie and Claret and Annette were thinking.

Had he dreamed it? Once, he was sure Annette had been curling a strand of hair around her finger and telling him with a wicked smile she might like to get into outlawing for a time. It paid well and threw in gunslinging, adventure, and a woman's independence to boot.

There were many dangers out there. He knew Athena would shoot him stone dead the moment she laid eyes on him. She'd enjoy it so much she'd likely shoot him seven or eight times. Probably shoot her daughters twelve or thirteen times because they were traitors. So, Valentina had cause to be jumpy.

Yet Roads would not relent till three days later—after he had cleaned out Budrow with brandy Valentina had in her saddlebags and seared the wounds shut—when Budrow roused himself and asked for water. They had precious little of it, but Roads gave it all to the no-good Yankee. He was confident there was a watering hole less than a day's ride ahead.

Val explained the shooting to Budrow and said she was sorry. Cut of a more forgiving cloth than Roads, he accepted her apology and let her sit beside him and talk. He watched the goings on between Roads and the two young women for an hour or two and shook his head.

"You're a ladies' man, Roads," he said, knowing the sisters heard him. "It's one of your strengths and one of your downfalls. The lady folk have had their way with you on this trail. Maybe Val too. I don't know. Nevertheless, let her be. I can see you have a bend toward her. That's probably why you're giving her such a hard time. If it had been Noon creeping in to slit our throats and do Athena's bidding, you'd have castigated Val for not shooting her outright. So, go easy."

"You have a fever," Roads retorted.

"Put your boots back in the stirrups and go easy."

Roads squatted by Budrow. "Thank you for your homily. You've got good color back. And some grit. But the color is probably from fever. Think you can sit your saddle? We can tie you in."

"I won't be the liveliest rattler in the nest, but I'll keep moving forward. I rode with a ball in me for two days after Buckers Tavern. We whipped you good there."

"You sound nasty, so I reckon you might as well get back up on Ranger. We've got to get to water. Want some jerky?"

"I'd probably throw it up."

"We'll not waste it then. I expect you're weak as a kitten."

"I'll hold my own."

"Rest a bit longer."

Roads stood up, hands on hips, and stared at Valentina. She still had some grit in her and faced his glare without expression, eyes flat, face set, and strong as stone.

"I did what I thought was best to save us," she said. "You would have done the same."

"No, I wouldn't have."

"Yes, you would have. Faster than me. And you'd have fired into the dark in case there were others too."

Roads grunted. "Get your guns and truck from Betsy. We're going for water. Help the Yankee into his saddle, both of you. And keep your eyes wide. There's bad blood all around us. Now the four of us are here together, I don't care who you shoot outside of our camp."

They followed animal tracks to the watering hole. Roads had never been there before, but he'd heard a few words about it and once memorized bits of an old torn up map. Budrow did not do particularly well. He rode like a sack of flour. Only Betsy riding beside him kept him upright. It took a while, despite animal tracks, to get to the water, tucked away as it was among a scramble of rocks and boulders and completely out of sight. But Val pointed them in the right direction and there it was, a small pool fed from under sand and stone, a fox running away from them as fast as it could. There was even some shade from a few scruffy trees.

"We'll stay here for now," Roads announced. "Water up a day or two. Let the Yankee gather up his fortitude."

"I thought you were in an all-fired hurry to get to your sister," growled Budrow.

"Let God Almighty work on the timing. I got some saying none of it's her fault. What happened back on the homestead was her husband to blame. But I got my head saying to me she's enjoying herself now. She likes the notoriety and the fame. She might even like the killing. I got a gut feeling she'll pull on me fast as a lightning storm. And I'll do the same. But I'm in no hurry to put a bullet in her brain. So, we'll water up here a couple of days."

Betsy was strong enough to ease Budrow out of his saddle and help him hobble over to a patch of shade with no one helping her. Then she filled his canteen and put it in his hand. Then she sat beside him, and they chatted.

At night, Roads did some chatting too. He surprised himself by gravitating to Valentina. Maybe he was still sore at her. But maybe he wasn't. He asked her what she felt about the trail ahead.

She shrugged, turning away from him. "Now you want my advice? I think Ma'll set an ambush. For all I know, she'll kill those three women friends of yours when she doesn't need their guns anymore."

"Will she kill my sister?"

"Who knows? Ma is wild as a mare stung by a wasp and just as wild. She's just as likely to join the gang. But also, just as likely to wanna be Boss Lady of the outlaws. Be the new Chica Bandida. In which case, she'd drill your sister."

"Unless Alice drilled Athena first."

"What's on your mind, ladies' man? Why are you sitting here with a desperado like me?"

"I'm thinking out loud."

"Go think out loud with someone else. Go think out loud with your horse. I'm not the next cowgirl in line anymore. You treated me like dirt. We're through. I have a mind to head out without you tomorrow. Why the heck should I ride with you anymore?"

"Betsy may have other ideas."

"Let her have them. If she wants to court a Yankee, fine. I don't need her. And I sure as heck don't need you."

Her pistol came up fast. Too fast for Roads. His Remington was out, but she would trigger before he would. She fired. He flinched as if he'd been hit. She fired again. A body fell into him like dead weight. He heard a string of curses in Spanish. It turned into gurgling and choking.

He twisted, and the body slid off him. The man had a bullet hole in his forehead and one eye shot out. Another man was on the ground burping blood and had a slit throat. Valentina was straddling him with her knife. But a third man pounced, got his fingers in her hair, ripped her head back and brandished his own enormous blade while he spewed Spanish like a kettle screaming steam. Roads fired three times and the man's head disappeared.

He tried to pierce the dark with his eyes. "There's someone else."

Betsy was with them. "There's no one else. I swear. I saw everything from the gun flashes. There's no one else."

"What is it?" asked Val, panting.

"*Bandidos*," Betsy told her.

Roads was still coiled, his pistol ready. "It makes no sense. Alice feeding her men to us to be killed piece by piece."

Valentina's face was white in the night, lit by a stroke of moonlight that came out from behind a small cloud. Her cheeks were streaked with jagged lines of blood. "It makes sense one way."

"What way?" hissed Roads.

"If your sister wanted you to think she was pretty much on her own now."

"So?"

"So, your guard would be down. Maybe The Ten are pretty much all dead. That doesn't mean she don't have a passel of new outlaws who have joined her gang over the past few weeks. She wants you to come now. Come fast and careless. And they'll be set to cut you down. These here were bait. She wants you rushing in, thinking she's defenseless."

Budrow spoke up in the dark. "She's making sense, Garrett. You Rebs pulled that on us more than once. Making it look like you were down to a half-dozen. We charge and there's a hundred of you firing your muskets at us."

Roads sat back on his heels. "I think we are close then."

"Very close," Budrow agreed.

"What about the sisters' momma bear?"

"I think she's close too. She may already be part of your sister's gang. These outlaw attacks are a good game for them. Alice rolls the dice, and maybe she's lucky. Maybe her men kill you. If not, you think she has hardly any guns left to protect her and lures you in, then you're trapped ... with twenty men and women you didn't count on. All shooting you up and us with you. She wins."

"She always did have to win the board games and sack races."

Roads and Val stayed up. The other two fell asleep nearby. When sunrise touched Val's face, she washed the blood off. She asked Roads if she'd got it all. He took her rag and dealt with a few patches she'd missed. Their faces were close.

They had moved away from the bodies during the night, as far as they could. Roads judged it to be two when they heard some snarling and crunching. Then the sound of bodies being dragged accompanied by more snarling. There was nothing to see in the morning but blood turned black and a chewed boot.

"What's next?" asked Val. "I suppose we just follow their tracks, and it will take us where they came from. Which is what they want."

Roads nodded and smoked. "I would say it has been all along. Those other bandidos from a couple of weeks ago were bait too. We are well on our way into my sister's trap. For all we know, she has twenty or twenty-five guns by now."

"The papers haven't said anything about that."

"We haven't seen a paper in weeks, Valentina. We have no idea what's going on, what trains or stages or banks they have robbed, how many people they have shot. We're completely in the dark."

"May I have one of those?"

"You may indeed. You saved my life."

"You saved mine."

★★★

Roads gave her one of his large cigars. She leaned toward him to share the flame of his match. Their faces touched. Both felt the shock zip through their bodies. Neither jerked away. She remained in place, puffing till she had the cigar exactly the way she wanted it. Then she smiled and blew smoke at him.

"See?" she teased. "You can be tamed, Granite."

"You think I'm tame?"

"Tamer than you were a week ago."

"I must apologize for my intemperance. I was in a rage, and I was cruel. You are right. If I'd spotted a skulking form, I'd have fired too. Considering our present circumstances."

"You ever wonder who the hunter is and who the hunted is now?" Val asked.

Roads snorted. "I do indeed. I reckon we are both."

CHAPTER 18

START THE BALL

Budrow healed up quick. His wounds had been bloody but not serious. Betsy wrapped him up tight and fed him hot soup made from a big desert tortoise she caught when it was coming down to the spring. After two days of no riding and plenty of sweet water from the rock, Budrow's blood was running again. On the morning of the third day, they rousted out in the chill, gray desert predawn, saddled up, and headed northwest. Budrow clambered up in his saddle with a grunt.

"Little stiff, Kit?" Roads grinned through cheroot smoke.

"Yes, but I'm wrapped up like an Egyptian mummy, so I can take the trail."

The trail of the men who had attacked them in the camp was plain, as though they had wanted the trackers to be very sure where they were going.

"They wanted us to know where they came from, Roads."

Garrett nodded. "Either that or they were all-fired sure they were going to kill us all. One thing we know. Alice and her gang will wait for us where those tracks started."

Valentina nodded. "That's for dang sure."

They halted their horses at the top of a small ridge. The trail led straight across the dusty bowl below them. Budrow looked at the girls. "What are you Coopers going to do when your ma comes riding at you with hell blasting from her shotgun? Duck and run? Shoot her off her horse? Switch sides? You better tell us quick, because I don't want to get back-shot by a pair of skunks that can't get their priorities straight."

Betsy and Valentina looked at each other but said nothing.

Garrett shook his head. "Where we are riding is no place for indecision. You're either with us or not. If you don't think you can shoot your siblings, you best just ride on ahead or go back. Now's the time to say."

Betsy swallowed hard. "I don't know, Roads."

Garrett turned to Valentina. "That's one. What about you, Val?"

Val grinned. "I ain't never been close to my ma. Betsy here got off light because she was the younger. I took all the whippings and the put-downs. Athena Cooper is just another woman to me. I would'a left home when I was twelve, but I had nowhere to go. And I meant what I said when I sent Stella off tied to her horse. I'll kill Ma quick if she messes with me, and she knows it.

Roads nodded at Betsy. "What about her? She seems indecisive. I watched ol' Bobby Lee stand in the same place at Gettysburg, and that decision lost him the war. If we ride together, we ride with one mind or quit now."

Val moved her horse closer to her sister and stared her right in the eyes. Betsy held her gaze for a minute and then dropped her eyes. Val spoke as she stared her sister down. "Betsy will ride with me and do what I say. Mostly 'cause she knows I'll whip her to brown butter if she steps one foot off my trail, then shoot the remains to ragdolls. Right, Bets?"

Betsy swallowed hard and nodded.

Val leaned closer. "And if I see you move one inch in the wrong direction, you'll be coyote feed, understand?"

Betsy nodded again.

Val wheeled her horse away from her sister. "Okay, fellas. Let's go, Betsy." She took off on a run, Betsy right on her heels, Budrow and Roads right behind.

★★★

Late in the afternoon, they crossed into New Mexico. The landscape had been changing from the playas and dusty ridges, and the land was rising. Ahead of them across a sage-covered waste loomed a long sawtooth ridge. Blue sky framed the razor-sharp peaks that rose out of a green carpet stretched from where they sat all the way to the base of the forbidding hills—green brought on by a few days of hard rain.

"Organ Mountains." Budrow shook his head. "*La Sierra de los Órganos.*"

Garret nodded. "That's where Oliver Loving ran into a band of Comanche that shot him full of arrows. Charlie took his body all the way back to his ranch to bury him. They were long-time pards."

Budrow took a swig of water from his canteen, rinsed his mouth, and spit. "You could hide ten thousand cows up in those hills. There are canyons upon canyons and trails leading right back to where you started after a day's hard ride. If that's where Alice and her gang are holed up, we got a hard ride ahead."

Dark clouds were forming above the stark range. Across the prairie, Budrow could see the tops of the sage moving.

"There's a front moving this way off those hills. Looks like we are in for some rain ... again."

Val spoke up. "We better find some cover."

Garrett nodded. "Yep. But keep your eyes and ears open. We may just cut your mama's trail. She'll be looking for cover too."

***

The rain was coming down, just enough to get them wet but not enough to be uncomfortable, when they came to a small side canyon. There were many deer tracks leading in and out, as well as coyote and one set of big lion tracks but no horse tracks.

Garrett pointed up at the canyon. "Must be water up there, a spring. Everybody's going up. Let's look it over. My canteen is empty, and we need a rest."

The riders turned their horses up the canyon. They rode for about an hour up a winding trail through the thick forest. The pines lining the trail slowly thinned, and fir and spruce replaced them. As they got higher, the trail broadened while the shadows darkened under the trees. Until at last, they topped a rise and looked down into a seneca, a park-like bowl hidden amid mighty peaks. They rode down out of the heavily timbered forest into a quiet meadow, knee high in lush grass. A broad stream crossed their path and tumbled down a shallow, rocky stretch into a quiet lake. Budrow turned them into the stream, and they rode down into the still water. The bottom was hard sand and packed gravel, and they did not leave any discernable tracks.

They rode silently around the edge of the quiet pool to where another stream tumbled down and disappeared down another cleft in the mountainside. Back under the trees was a flat area with some deadfalls under the trees.

Budrow turned Ranger, and they climbed the shallow bank. "This looks good. We'll pull those dead logs into a bulwark and sleep behind it. No fire, though. We still don't know where everybody is."

★★★

Early in the morning, as the gray was surrendering to the first pale blue of dawn, Granite awoke. Something was different in the sounds of the night. He heard it again, a slight splash, someone or something walking in the water down at the lake. He reached over and touched Budrow on the shoulder. Instantly, his friend was awake. Granite put a finger to his lips, then pointed to the lake. They quickly scooted to where the girls lay and woke them. Val came awake quietly with a pistol in her hand. Betsy started to say something, but Budrow clapped his hand over her mouth.

"We got visitors," Granite whispered.

They crawled back to the logs they had piled up the night before and peered through the cracks. Budrow saw the silhouette of a rider against the pale dawn, then another, then another until he counted four in all.

Then a quiet voice came to their ears.

"I can't tell if they climbed out, Alice."

A woman's voice. "Garrett's too good to leave a trail. If he came out of the lake, we'll never see it in this light. We'll ride on to the hideout. If he wants to follow, it's on his head. Grimsby will be waiting with five new men. Better we meet him there than wait until sunup and shoot it out with us in the open and him down behind some rocks. Mrs. Roads didn't raise any dumb kids."

Garret's heart jumped. His sister was not more than fifty yards away with the remains of her gang. Garrett felt something move next to him. Valentina was drawing a bead on the lead rider. Suddenly, the muzzle of Garrett's gun was against the side of Val's head.

"Not from ambush," he whispered. "Let them pass."

Val's gun came down. The riders moved down the lake. They heard the click of horses' hooves on rock as they rode out by the shallow stream left by the other exit to the senaca. Soon the sound of the riders was swallowed up by the walls of the small cleft that was the way out.

Val cussed. "You should have let me shoot her."

"Why? How you gonna get her body down the hill to collect the reward, especially when I'm standing over it? You know, Val, life is hard, but it's even harder if you're stupid."

Val flushed red. "You calling me stupid?"

"Yeah. You shoot Alice out of the saddle, we get in a gunfight with her men and the riders coming down the swale on the other side of the lake ride up and finish us all off."

"Riders? What ...?"

Garret put his hand over her mouth. "Just listen and stop shooting off your mouth. You got a lot to learn."

They lay quietly, and Budrow pointed. Sure enough, a group of riders were coming over the rise and down to the lake.

Coop's voice floated to them through the gray light. "They rode down the stream and went into the lake, Mama."

"Good. We got them now. We'll just follow them right to their hideout. Midnight, Noon, you keep a watch in case Roads and them traitorous whelps come ridin' up. Don't want to get between a rock and a hard place."

The group rode into the lake—Coop, his brother, Athena, Annette, Claret, and Nettie. Back a ways, Midnight and Noon kept watch.

Roads whispered to Val and Betsy. "Let them ride too. We don't have enough firepower to challenge them. Alice said they have five new men waiting at their camp. Let Athena ride into the mess. We'll be right behind to cleanup. And you're not stupid, Val, just too darned impetuous."

They watched as Athena's crew rode past. When they were safely gone, Budrow breathed a sigh of relief. "They didn't know we came up here first. Alice's boys must have ridden over our tracks and wiped them out."

Roads nodded. "There's only one tracker I know who could have spotted our tracks among Alice's—Claret Black. Her not giving us away is very encouraging to me. That means she's either doing this under protest, or she's just biding her time." Garrett climbed over the log and strode down to the lake. Right at the point where they had ridden out, he found what he was looking for—a glass marble lying on the sand, the one he'd given Claret when they were kids. He grinned. Picking up the marble, he walked back to the camp.

★★★

After they had a quick breakfast, the four riders saddled up and rode out. The trail down the canyon was narrow and treacherous but not too steep. They came out at the bottom in about two hours. A trail of tracks led off to the northwest down a narrow valley. The mountains rose sharply on either side. The morning was making itself known among the peaks, and the first golden rays of the sun were filtering into the shadows where they rode.

"Alice knows she's being trailed, but she thinks it's me. Athena will follow them to their hideout and try to hold them up. The woman has an itch for the reward and to have her own gang. What she doesn't know is there are nine guns waiting, not four. It won't matter to Alice who rides in. She's trail-savvy and dangerous. You corner her in her den and you're in for trouble."

Two hours later, they came to a trail that led up over a ridge. Budrow held up a hand, and they stopped. "I'm betting over that ridge is Alice's hideout. Athena probably left her horses somewhere up in that bunch of trees, and the girls are creeping down to the camp. I think the ball is about to begin."

And begin it did.

CHAPTER 19

JOKERS WILD

April 1865

"The word I have is the general intends to surrender the Army of Northern Virginia to Grant."

Roads nodded. "We've all heard, Colonel Sten."

"Do you have the general's ear?"

"Of course not."

"Do you think we can break through?"

Roads's eyes narrowed in the dimming light of dusk so they were almost black. "The general has tried many times. The boys are game. But the odds are stacked against us. There are too many Yankees. They are a brick wall of blue."

"Then it's my last chance to exact revenge and get cleanly away with it. I need your help, Roads."

"Revenge? Against whom? The Yankees?"

"One of our own. A Confederate officer. He betrayed me at Campers Forge. Withdrew our left flank in the face of a cavalry assault. Our line crumbled. They slaughtered us. But he still lives and breathes and drinks his bourbon. He is only three fires to our left."

"What exactly is it you want me to do?"

"Draw him out. Away from his tent and his men. You know Skerritt, don't you?"

"What? Major Skerritt? We go back to Antietam."

"Then he'll come out to you."

"What are your intentions, Colonel?"

"When you bring him away from the fire, I'll gut the traitor like a trout."

"My Lord, Major, do you seriously expect me to be party to that?"

"I'm not asking. It's an order. I outrank you."

Roads protested. "You can't order me to help you murder a Confederate officer."

Sten's face was granite. "I can. I am. This is a court martial followed by a just execution. No one will miss him with the turmoil over the general's surrender."

"Of course, they'll miss him."

A pistol barrel pressed into Roads's stomach. "No one will miss you, either. If you don't do as I ask, I'll kill you here and now and swear I saw a Yankee marauder do you in. If you approach Skerritt, and I see you've warned him, I'll shoot you both dead from the shadows. You know I'm a crack pistol shot."

"You won't get away with that."

"I will. Do you have any idea how much our men hate Skerritt? They want him dead as much as I do."

"Then ask one of them to help you spill his blood," argued Roads. "Why do you want me?"

"Because he trusts you," Sten replied. "He will step toward the dark with you. I will make it quick, Roads. But not painless." Sten prodded Roads with his pistol again. "Get on with it. Remember, I'll be watching. And know this, I've killed so many men, I don't even feel it anymore. But I will have Skerritt's head this night."

In the end, in the midnight dark, Roads had turned the tables on Colonel Sten, then slipped his body into a fast-flowing creek. No one found him.

★★★

The harsh memory made a man think. Roads stared into the dark. "*Budrow*," he whispered.

Budrow was nearby. He crawled over. "What is it?" he asked softly.

"Am I betraying my sister?"

"What?"

"We are going to trap them. Shoot them. I may put a bullet through my sister's skull. As if it's war. I want to protect my family's honor by killing a member of my family?"

Budrow said nothing.

"Is this a good thing I do?" asked Roads.

"She's a gunslinger now, Roads. An outlaw. How many you reckon she's shot dead?"

"I wouldn't know."

"Would you rather I do her in?"

"No, sir, I would not. It's just with the likelihood of the deed upon me, I hesitate at killing one of my own. My very own."

"Understood."

"There was a time we were children at play. A time before the war, we worked the cattle together. Mended fences. Branded. Castrated young bulls. Doctored. Calved. We did everything, Budrow."

Roads saw him nod slowly, his eyes dark and tight.

Roads sighed as if he'd given up and rubbed a hand into his face for several long seconds. "I've been dealt a bad hand. Darned if I do and darned if I don't."

"They're hunting us now, like we're hunting them. It would be good to get in the first blow."

"It would. It would indeed, Yank." Roads looked around in the night. "Where's Valentina?"

A voice spoke up quietly. "Right here, Colonel. With Betsy."

"We will require four fires. One large. They will dismiss that one. Two others progressively smaller they think might be ours. Then a fourth, barely coals. They will track each of them. Maybe even fire into the dark."

"Where will we be?" asked Valentina.

"In the blackness. But I'll make sure they spot me hiding. It's up to you all to pick them off the moment they take me."

"What if they just up and shoot you where you stand?"

"I'm counting on your mother being part of the group hunting us tonight. And your mother will want to gloat awhile before she kills me. Though I'm certain she'll be required to bring me alive to my sister. Listen. This ploy worked on the blue bellies at Jarod's Ferry. We bagged all ten without a loss. I hope we may have similar good fortune now."

"That's it?" Valentina questioned him. "That's the plan? Four fires? And you're the bait?"

"It comes down to a matter of trust. I trusted my men at Jarod's Ferry. Indeed, I trusted them with my life. But they were men who'd fought beside me for years. I know I can trust Budrow, no-good Yankee though he is. Can I trust you and your sister?"

"Of course you can."

"I've been betrayed more than once on this ride. The ladies have outplayed me at every turn. They've had aces high and Jokers wild. They've showed me the Queen of Hearts while they had the Queen of Spades up their pretty sleeves."

"I know. And I'm convinced they are happy, ready, and in excited anticipation of outwitting you again. Another feather in their hats. There will be a bushwhack. They will cry out for your help and strike with the knife or gun. That is their scheme. I know it is. But not me, sir. Not me."

"Not yet."

"Not ever."

Roads smiled. Val was convincing. But the others had been too—Sin, Noon, Nettie, Claret Black, Annette—they had all played winsome and alluring hands of hearts and diamonds, spreading their cards on the clean green felt, eyes betraying nothing but beauty, charm, and doe-eyed innocence. Even Athena had pulled this off at one time or another. All of them made him feel safe and protected in their presence—just before they pistol whipped Roads or put the boots to him or hogtied his body hand and foot. Each incident was painfully branded in his memory. They'd turned out royal flushes to his deuces. What was supposed to be a trail to return honor to his family name had become a trail of dishonor for him each time they'd made sure he played the fool, their laughter ringing in his ears. The humiliations still stuck in his craw. He was not sure how to clear them. The Lord knew what further disgrace and discomfort they held in store for him after being bent to his sister's wild will at her hideout.

He came out of his reverie and stared into Val's strong eyes. "We'll see. But yes, I am the bait, Val. I will sit just apart from the fire of coals, looking as if I am lurking and hoping to ambush them. Then, I will let them ambush me. So, now, light the fires. I will take care of my bed of coals. And when you shoot, don't hesitate. Acquire your targets and cut them down. This is war. Can I count on you, Val?"

"Yes."

"Even to put your own mother in your sights?"

"Yes."

"Godspeed then. Budrow, Val, Betsy, stay sharp."

Roads reckoned it might work. He also knew he might have figured it wrong—then he'd be dead in a few minutes. He had been double-crossed again and again on this trail. Yet strangely enough, he did not think Val would turn her gun on him. It was Betsy who was the wild card.

He did not make a large fire like the others produced. He no sooner ignited some wood and tinder with a match, one of the few he had left in his pocket, than he extinguished it, leaving only a handful of coals glimmering orange and red. Afterwards, he moved away and crouched, to all appearances, a man waiting to pounce. But he knew, setting himself up, they would spot him before he spotted anyone else, and he was the prey, not the hunter.

After only a few minutes, Roads sensed another person was behind him. It was not an animal. It was human. He waited for a bullet to the brain, a deadly whisper and threat, a knife's whetted edge to his throat. Or, with luck, a swift shot from Budrow or Valentina straight to his enemy's heart. But the first thing that happened was a shout more like a scream.

"Watch out, Ma! It's a trap!"

It was Betsy's cry. Practically simultaneous with her shriek of warning, there was a gunshot and Roads saw her body fall into the large fire. Valentina was just at the edge of the flames, her face contorted into a mask of rage and hate. Her Winchester was in her hands, a wisp of gun smoke, barely visible, twisting from the barrel's mouth.

"Here I am, Ma, you miserable wretch! Come and get some!" Val snapped off four shots at Roads's back. "Take it all! All my love!" She fired quickly three more times. The muzzle flame was long and yellow and wicked.

Roads heard a loud grunt of pain. A body fell against him. An ice-cold barrel ground into his neck. It seemed to him he had never felt anything as cold, not even a north wind, not even a blast of snow.

"I curse you for turning my girl against me." It was Athena's voice, and it was heavy with agony and hurt. The sticky flow of blood was soaking into his shirt. "I ain't going to hell alone ... Mister High and Mighty ... blowing you to pieces is the best gift ... I can give the world on my way out ... your sister wants you in one piece to dispose of at her leisure ... but that's a promise my pleasure to break."

Gunfire erupted all around him, orange and yellow flashes burning the darkness. Roads heard yelling in Spanish. In the firelight, he suddenly saw Val leap onto a bearded man's back, knock off his sombrero, yank his head back by the hair to expose his throat, then slit it open with a swift sweep of her blade. She fell with him when he collapsed, scrambling to her feet to kick him, spit, and swing quickly to her right, pull her pistol, and fire into the night. Roads saw another man collapse under the weight of her fierce gunfire. Afterwards, she vanished out of the light, but Roads could see her left sleeve was black with blood.

The barrel of Athena's gun had never left his neck. Her body was still there too, slumped against him, sliding down his back, getting closer and closer to the ground. She fired. Her hand jerked to the left and the shot cut his neck, but did no more damage than that, though the miss stung like a swarm of wasps. She fired again, but her hand did not have a strong grip. Roads felt the barrel flip and the bullet bite into his boot.

Athena cursed and curled an arm that still had plenty of strength in it around his throat. The tip of a knife pricked the small of his back.

"I ain't no ... good for this world anymore, Mister Roads," she gasped out with a tremendous effort. "But ... praise God and the Devil ... neither are you."

She thrust the knife home with all she had left.

CHAPTER 20

HONOR'S PRICE

The fires were lit. Budrow thumbed cartridges into his Colts and slipped into the darkness of some Manzanita scrub. He could see Roads crouched by the coals of his small fire, a lion, waiting for the hyenas to swarm him. Suddenly, Betsy's scream cut through the night.

"Watch out, Ma! It's a trap!"

Almost before the cry had stopped echoing off the rocks, he heard Valentina's howl of rage and the heavy roar of her Winchester tore the night. Betsy's shriek cut short as Val blasted her sister into a traitor's hell. Budrow wanted to help Roads, but suddenly there were shadows around him, and he knew he was in a fight.

In the darkness, a six-gun flowered flaming death. Budrow felt a tug at his sleeve and then he was returning fire and running. An inarticulate cry from the darkness, another blossom of flame and bullets swarmed around him like angry bees. He fired straight at the flames. Another yell, a death scream, and he knew he had taken out two.

He threw himself down behind an outcrop of rocks, but did not stay, knowing the only way he would survive was to keep moving. He rolled over and snapped another shot at a shadow. This time the scream was a woman.

I hope that wasn't Nettie.

Now Budrow was running. Something stuck out in front of him... a leg... before he could dodge it, the leg caught his and he tumbled and rolled. As he did, he felt a slug tear through his hat.

I'll thank God for that leg later.

He saw someone ... a man turning toward him. Budrow lunged up, his Colt caught the man on the side of the head, and he went down in a heap. He knelt down to the one who had tripped him. A flash of red hair.

"Nettie?"

She was lying with a gag in her mouth and her hands behind her. Budrow rolled her over and cut the leather thong holding her wrists with his Bowie. He was going for the gag when he saw her eyes open wide and look beyond him. He heard a boot crunch on gravel. He threw himself to the side as the boot crunched down where his backbone had been. Budrow scissored the leg, and the man went down hard.

Quick as a cat, Budrow was on his feet, but so was the man. A big, brutal-looking man with heavy shoulders and unshaven face. He grinned at Budrow as they circled, looking for an opening.

He's got sixty pounds on me. Hope he doesn't know about boxing.

Budrow feinted, and the big man lunged. He ran face-first into a stabbed right hand, followed by a left to the ear. The man grunted, shook his head, and came up grinning.

Suddenly he heard Granite's Colts blast, followed by another scream, this time a man.

Valentina's rifle coughed, and another man yelled.

That's five.

The man he was facing dove at him, grabbing his legs and taking him down. As Budrow fell, he hooked his opponent in the face, stabbing into his eyes. The man screamed. Budrow jerked the enormous head away and jammed the butt of his palm under the big boy's chin. For a moment they strained and then Budrow jerked his hand away and hit him in the Adam's apple. He jerked back, choking and gasping, and Budrow heaved him off.

Granite's guns roared again. Then Budrow saw another man coming out of the dark. His opponent grabbed up a gun. Budrow grabbed for his left-hand Colt, but the two had him boxed. Suddenly, the darkness beside him blossomed red death. The first man spun away, and the second man swung his gun to Budrow's left. But not before Budrow's left-hand Colt snaked out of the holster and delivered two lead messengers straight into the swarthy man's throat.

He turned. Nettie was standing beside him, still gagged but pistoled up. Her eyes lit up and then they heard running. Val charged past.

"Granite's down. Let's get them."

The three of them ran toward Roads's fire. Two more men were advancing on Roads who lay stretched out on the ground, thumbing cartridges into his Colt.

"Drop 'em or die," yelled Val. The two men spun, guns rising.

"Coop?" Val hesitated for just a split second.

The first man's gun belched flame and a bright red flower blossomed on Val's shirt front. Coop spun and put a slug right behind the man's ear. He ran to his sister's side. Val was stretched out, a bloody froth already spraying from her lips.

"I'm lung-shot, Coop. I'm a goner."

"Val, I'm sorry. I didn't know ..."

Coop dropped his gun and raised his hands. "I'm out of it, Budrow. My word."

Budrow nodded. "See to your sister, then."

Budrow looked at the battlefield. He could see some bodies, and there was no more gunfire.

Looks like the ball is over ...

Nettie was already kneeling at Granite's side. Budrow walked over. His friend was pale.

"How ya doing Roads? You okay?"

Granite grinned. His face was pale, but there was no death in his eyes. "I should smile. I'm okay. Take more than a knife in the side and a shoulder shot to take me out." Nettie had pulled open his shirt. There was a hole high on his shoulder that had bled pretty good, and the side of his shirt was soaked in blood. The side of his neck had a nasty powder burn and a bullet cut.

"When Athena came up behind me, I thought I was a gone gosling. She put the gun right in my ear, and just like I thought, she did a bit of crowing before she shot me. If Betsy hadn't screamed, I'd be ready for Boot Hill. As it was, Val shot Betsy then shot her ma. Athena pushed a knife into my back while she was dyin', but she hit my cartridge belt and slid off. Burned like Hades, but she didn't get me."

Roads looked up at Nettie, who was tearing strips off her shirt and making bandages.

"Where did you get this one?"

"She was lying trussed up like a market hog. I was dancing with two fellers, and she reached out and tripped me just before the fella behind me shot my head off. Timely."

Budrow put his hand on Nettie's shoulder. "Why'd you save me, Major Paris?"

Nettie looked up at Budrow. Her eyes were sad, but there was a grin on her face. "Guess I just tired of being bossed around by a woman who knew less than I do. I told her so, and she tied me up."

"Where are the other girls?"

"Annette and Claret rode out after we caught Garret and Val and Betsy back at the canyon. I don't know where they are. Claret left you her marble, you know, back there when you were hidden by the lake. She wanted you to know that she ... she remembered. I stayed around to see if I could thwart Athena's plans. You know Alice is my friend."

Budrow nodded. "Well, it seems you did. We better go see what's up. Granite, you rest easy."

They walked together. Athena was dead, along with Betsy. Five of the remaining ten were dead. By a clump of cholla, they came upon Midnight and Noon. Sindy was cradling Faye in her arms. Faye was dead. Sindy looked up.

"Howdy, Budrow, Nettie. My sister's dead." Her voice was matter of fact, but her face was not.

Budrow remembered the woman's scream he had heard when he fired into the dark, but he said nothing.

"Are you done then?"

Sindy sighed. "Yeah, I think so. She was all I had. Don't know what I'll do without her." The hard lines of her face broke, and she bent over Faye and wept.

Nettie stroked Sindy's hair. "Y'all should go back to New Orleans, Sindy. This west is a hard place for women who want to ride with men, to be better than men. It took me a while to figure that out"

She looked up at Budrow, and for the first time in a long time, he saw Nettie Paris. "I don't want to do it anymore. I don't want to punch cows or chase rustlers or ride with an all-girl gang. I need someone to take care of me. Someone like you, Kit."

Budrow nodded. "I know, Nettie."

★★★

They left Sindy and walked around the camp. All the Coopers, except Coop and Val, were dead, and Val was going. Four of the five men left from The Ten were dead as well. They looked around, but they couldn't find Alice or the last man. They had escaped.

Budrow and Nettie walked back to where Cooper was sitting with Val. Val was dead. Cooper looked up. "I should never have got into this mess, but I could never stand up to Ma."

Budrow took out his Colt and thumbed cartridges into the empty chambers. "What are you going to do, Coop?"

"I'm riding back to Longhorn. We still got a store and the homestead. Never should have left. I'm out of all this. You won't see me again, Budrow."

Budrow spun the colt and slid it into his holster. "Okay, Coop. I'll take your word. But know this. If I find you on my trail ever, or if I ever cut yours, you better come shooting. Because I will."

"Understood, Budrow. Now let's get these folks buried."

★★★

The morning sun was just breaking through the gray predawn when they finished digging. The sandy soil had made it easy. Sindy had ridden out, unable to watch her sister put in the dirt. The four Coopers, Faye, and the four from Alice's gang were laid side by side. Budrow looked up at the land. The Tularosa Basin paled away into the distance, a feast of open land, biting air and clear blue skies. Far off, the rising sun glinted off pure white dunes.

Behind them the arid Organ Mountains rose in splendor. Granite sat propped up against a rock.

"It's a lovely place, Kit. I guess if I was to cash in my chips, I'd like a valley like this to look over."

Cooper nodded. "We was coming down on Alice when you all showed up. Ma said we was to get you first. She was set on gettin' you dead, Colonel Roads. I didn't know who I was shooting at for a while. Seems like everybody took some losses."

Granite nodded. "Alice was probably laughing, although she's shy four of her gang. Didn't find her?"

Budrow shook his head. "Nope, just Coopers and the four owlhoots. Alice is gone with one of her gang."

Cooper took his hat off. "Can you say a few words, Colonel?"

Granite swept off his hat. "Me and God ain't been seeing eye to eye for a while, so I will defer to my more cultivated friend. Budrow?"

Budrow took his hat in his hands. "O God, who gave us birth, you are ever more ready to hear than we are to pray. You know our needs before we ask and our ignorance in asking. Give to us now your grace, as we shrink before the mystery of death, wc may see the light of eternity. Help us live as those who are prepared to die. And when our days here are accomplished, enable us to die as those who go forth to live, so that living or dying, our life may be in you. Amen."

Budrow, Cooper, and Nettie began throwing dirt in the graves. Granite pulled out a cheroot.

"My last one."

Nettie looked up. "I hear a horse."

They stopped and waited. The horse came closer.

"Hello, the camp. My hands are empty. Can I ride in? I have a message for Roads."

Roads stood. "Come on in ... but remember to keep your hands in plain sight."

"Don't want no trouble. Just the messenger."

A man on a buckskin horse came through the mesquite and pulled up in front of them. His hands were up, and he did not wear a gun.

"Which one of you is Roads?"

Granite stepped forward.

The man handed Roads a piece of paper. "This here is from Alice. I came as a favor to you and her. I'd like safe passage to ride out."

"You got it, friend. But you better light a shuck. The next time we meet might be a little more unpleasant."

"Will do."

The man turned his horse and rode away.

Garret opened the paper. He read it, then folded it and put it in his shirt pocket.

"What's up, Granite?"

"Alice wants to meet, just her and me. To work this out. I reckon I better go."

CHAPTER 21

BLACK ALICIA

Roads took his time.

Every rock and every cleft in a rock could hide a shooter. But he had no intention of creeping along in the dark. If Alice had set up an ambush, so be it. He'd fight his way out like he had a score of times during the war. His sense was there would be no ambush. His sister would not double cross him. She may not cotton to his way of thinking, but they would talk. There had always been talk between them.

He had not ridden two hours before he was hailed. It was still early and a little cold. Only six. The sun was up and held an edge to the sky like a knife. The voice came from behind him. "I could cut you open and let the buzzards pick over your breakfast." It was a man.

Roads stopped Sharpsburg but didn't turn around. "They won't be happy with it. All I've had is coffee. No cream. No sugar."

The man laughed. "You're like me. I can never eat till the sun sets and it cools off."

"I'm much the same."

"Just set there and keep your hands on the saddle. Your sister will be here soon."

She appeared in front of Roads on a black stallion, just as if she'd come out of the morning sky. "Garrett."

He doffed his slouch hat. "Alice."

She was dressed in all black—boots, pants, belt, gloves, shirt, her sombrero *cordobés* with a wide, flat brim. Even her face was burnt black from the sun. Only the silver conchos on the stallion's bridle held any light. And Alice's dark eyes.

She did not look anything like the ranch wife and sister she had once been. Roads took note of the broadness in her shoulders, the rough lines cut into her face, the muscles in her hands. She seemed taller. Maybe she was.

"Was it worth it?" she demanded, her voice harsh. "Trailing me?"

"Depends on how it ends." Roads kept his own voice mild.

"A lot of bodies."

"I know it."

"I hear you've been pistol whipped."

"More than once."

"By the fairer sex. And the stronger one."

"I shall give them a wide berth in the future."

She laughed, and her teeth were white in her darkness. "I won't live to see the day. Ladies are your gin and tonic. And your Achilles heel."

"I don't deny it."

She was smiling. "I know you think I'm all used up. I'm not. My gang is more than you know. Almost all women now. Except for Bud there and Jim who has his Yellowboy sighted on your thick skull. The gals voted to keep the pair."

"I see."

"You don't see. This is my life now. This is my freedom. Not too much a woman can do nowadays and be free. This is one way." She removed her sombrero and shook out her hair. It was as black and shiny as her stallion's mane and tail and hung down past her waist. "Ain't cut it since I lit out from the ranch. Don't intend to neither. This lifestyle suits me, Garrett."

"So it seems."

"Listen now, Brother. Don't believe the *Daily News* out of Galveston or the ugly Yankee *New York Times*. I killed two vigilantes and one lawman, and all three needed it. But that's it. I roughed up a few men and hung one, but he was part of my gang and a traitor. I did y'all a favor."

Roads nodded waiting for more.

"I killed the rat too—my husband. I should've shot Joby the day we tied the knot or cut his throat in bed. He killed my boy, Garrett. The skunk lost the ranch in a poker game and then laughed in my face. When I went for my gun, he tried to shoot me. He was going to put a bullet in me, but Jimmy threw himself in the way and took the bullet instead. I lost my mind after that. Jumped Joby and beat the living tar out of him. Then, I took his pistol and drilled him. Should've dragged him to death behind my horse. He didn't rate a bullet. You likely heard the skunk lost the ranch in a poker game. I robbed a Yankee pay wagon by myself and bought the ranch back for you. That's God's truth. No one knew it was me. I was dressed up like a man. Otherwise, that'd be another story to add to my Chica Bandida legend. I don't mind the legend, even though most of it is no truer than Rip Van Winkle. It helps when it comes to robbing and thieving. People see it's me, and their hands go up fast."

"Well, you didn't kill him, Alice. He stayed alive just long enough to feed the sheriff a cock and bull story about how you killed the boy first and then shot him. That's how this whole mess got started."

Alice shrugged. "Bad luck. I should have put the pistol between his eyes and blown his brains out the back of his head. He looked mighty dead when I rode out."

"How did you come to join up with The Ten? They're murderers."

"They were murderers. I don't guess we got one left alive. It was a necessity, brother. I used my robbery of the pay wagon to get in with them. I had to outshoot one hombre to prove my mettle, and pig stick another in a knife fight, but none of that was any trouble. A little while later, I cut down the leader when he insulted me. *Madre mía*, he was not only foul, but slow. After that, I was the boss. Only one man contested it. He was no trouble, neither. Since then I've been sittin' high and mighty ... and comfortable."

"What are your intentions?"

She laughed and her laugh was full of scorn. "To ride off and leave you alive, Garrett. I ain't coming back with you, and I ain't changing careers. What I'm asking from y'all? Just leave me be. I'll only kill them that needs killing and as for the gold and silver and bank notes? Why, we've already funded two orphanages in Texas with the leftovers."

"I heard that."

"We'll fund more. It's better than the Yankee government has done for the young 'uns the war left behind. So, just leave me be, Brother. I'll be wild. But I'll be good and wild."

"You know I'm bound to follow you."

She shook her head, and her black hair was like a raven's wings. "This ain't no dime western with *The Blazing Guns of Granite Roads* as the title. It's my book. My life will go my way."

Roads nodded. "There already is a book."

"Five. We even let a tinhorn ride with us for a couple of days so he could write another one. *The Woman in Black.* See it?"

"Not yet."

"Only a nickel. He gave me lovers. They all do now. I don't mind. They're closer to the truth than they know." Alice put the sombrero back on her head as the sun rose higher and heated the air. She didn't tuck her hair, but let it hang loose down to her hips. "Don't follow me, Brother. This is my story now. My ride. My trail. Not yours."

She whistled. Roads wondered what it was a signal for. A minute went by. He and his sister stared at one another. Alice was still as a stone. Riders appeared on the bluffs and crags that surrounded the trail. Some came down to sit their horses next to Alice. There were a lot of them, and they had bandannas pulled up under their eyes. They looked tough and lean and dangerous. They were all women. His sister grinned.

"Surprised? Well, whatever a man can do my gals can do twice as well, heck, ten times as well. Don't follow me, Garrett. I give the word, and they'll cut you up with their whips and hang you so high and loose you'll dance for an hour." One of the women next to her, hair as crimson as blood, lit a cigarette she had rolled and gave it to Alice. She put it in her mouth and drew on it, long and heavy. She blew the smoke at Roads. "Leave me be and we'll both live a long life. You can keep track of me in the papers. That'll suffice. We've got a female reporter with us for a week. She'll give us a new name now that we're rid of most of the men. Black Alicia. The Black Alicia Gang. Or whatever other title they give us that suits. I like it when the people name us—the farmers and ranchers and townsmen and their women. We make their lives more exciting. They love us, and they love reading about us. You know that, don't you, Garrett? So, don't take away their joy. They'll hate y'all for it if you try. Leave well enough alone. Turn around and go home. Stay there and rebuild the ranch. I'll visit you sometime. Yes, I will certainly do that. Do we understand one another?"

"I reckon we do."

"All right then. *Adios*."

"*Adios*, my sister."

She touched her fingers to the brim of her sombrero and turned her horse. Her women turned with her. In a few moments, they were gone, and Roads was alone. There wasn't even dust.

Roads had kept the Remington Val had gifted him in its holster. But when he heard the snap of a hoof on rocks, he wheeled his horse and aimed, ready to shoot. A tall woman in a tweed riding outfit, hat as flat as a griddle cake, reared her mount back, her eyes springing wide.

"Don't shoot!" she cried.

Roads did not lower the Remington. He spotted the silver pistol in a black holster on her hip. "Who are you? What's this?"

"I am ... I am Mandy Scott, sir. Out of Galveston. I work for the *Daily News*. I also write novels. I've published ten. Your sister detached me from her party."

"Detached you?"

"I am writing a piece on her gang. Her all-female gang ... or nearly so. She asked me to spend an hour with you and get her growing-up story."

"What is a growing-up story?" growled Roads, his voice as deep and dark as it had ever been. After hearing what Alice intended to do with the rest of her life, he was in no mood.

"Why, what she was like as a girl," Mandy explained, her nerves making her talk too fast. "Did she play with dolls? Did she play with ponies? Did she play with guns?"

"What? Ma'am, you make less sense the more you talk."

"Miss Scott."

"Miss Scott," Roads repeated, inclining his head. "I expect the public will want to hear she shot the ears off corn stalks at a hundred paces. That she climbed trees. Outwrestled all the boys and outran them too. Drank hard liquor at twelve."

"I don't know."

"In fact, she liked dresses and skirts, adored her doll collection, found boys repulsive, and liquor made her sick to her stomach."

"I see."

"I can only recall one event that would suit you and put Alice at the head of an outlaw gang."

"Alicia," Mandy corrected him.

Roads ignored her intervention. "A boy twice her age and twice her size kicked our puppy, Bobby. I intended to deal with it. But I did not have the opportunity. Alice was at him like a wild cat. She jumped on his back and pummeled his face with her fists. He collapsed under her, and she continued to lay into him as he groveled in the dirt and cried, '*Mercy! Mercy!*' She harbored no inclination to extend any mercy to him. Alice was a proper blue norther. I had to use all my strength to haul her off and hold her back. Even then, she got in a final kick to his head, and she was wearing spurs. It knocked him cold. He was an unholy mess. After sending Alice into the house, I fetched a bucket of water and tossed it on him. There wasn't much he could do. How would he be able to tell the ranching families a girl had beaten him up? So, he invented a cock and bull story about being thrown from a fast horse and dragged by the stirrup. I advanced this as an explanation of his sorry state as well. But, as these things always play out, everyone found out the truth. From then on, he was always called Mercy-Mercy. He ran away. But I did see him again. At Bull's Run. We both fought there."

Mandy was scribbling notes with a pencil. Roads had no doubt what he'd related would provide the lion's share of content for Alice's growing up story.

"Miss Scott," he ventured as she continued to write.

"Mmm?"

"Perhaps you'd be so good as to tell me who has been following us, slipping their mounts from bluff to bluff?"

Mandy did not look up. "Comanche."

"Comanche?"

"Our Comanche girls. Or rather, Alicia's Comanche girls. Nadua and Topsannah."

"And their purpose is to keep an eye on you?"

Head still down, Mandy snorted. "Their purpose is to keep an eye on you, sir. And if they don't much like what you do, to kill you and leave you to rot. Maybe bring back your head." She suddenly looked up and flashed a smile at Roads. "It would make a great story."

CHAPTER 22

THE HONOR TRAIL

Budrow heard him coming long before he rode in. And Ranger heard him before Budrow did. The horse had been grazing on some bunchgrass when he lifted his head, and his ears went forward. A few minutes later, the soft fall of horses' hooves could be heard in the sand. Budrow put his hand on his Colt.

"Roads?"

"It's me. Put your gun away."

Budrow grinned and whirled the pistol back into its holster. "Coffee's hot, and Nettie had some sugar in a sock in her saddlebags."

"Sounds good. Any breakfast going? Smells like somethin's baking."

"Nettie's got some biscuits in the oven. We scrounged up a little flour and a piece of dried deer meat. We've either got to find a town or head back down the trail."

Roads slid off Sharpsburg and stretched. "Well, I think it's option two."

"Leave? But what about Alice?"

"Alice told me what happened back at the ranch—how Joby gambled away the property and then tried to shoot her when she intervened. Joby killed the boy, not Alice. Jimmy jumped in between them to save his ma. She, being the hot-blooded Roads woman that she is, beat Joby senseless and then shot him twice to finish the job. Too bad she didn't."

Nettie looked up from her biscuits. "Do you believe her, Garrett?"

"Alice never lied to me in her whole life. I knew Joby to be a skunk, but it never occurred to me he would actually gamble the ranch away. But ..."

Budrow glanced at Roads. "But what?"

"Like I said. Alice never told me an untruth, even when she was in the wrong. I'd trust her with my life."

Budrow got a forked stick and lifted the Dutch oven off the coals. "So, pard, are we done here?"

Roads pulled a cheroot from his pocket and struck a match. "I think we rode this river to its mouth, Kit."

★★★

Thirty days later—to the day—Budrow, Nettie, and Roads rode up to the old Roads Ranch on the Canadian. The burned-down house had fallen in on itself, but the bunkhouse was still standing. A few broken panes marred the windows along the front, and shredded curtains flapped weakly in the open frames. It was the beginning of October, and a chilling wind drove their collars up around their necks. Long grass and dead leaves filled what used to be Alice's well-tended garden. The rocking chair where Alice spent her knitting time still stood on the remains of the front porch and creaked in the wind. The first thing Roads did was ride to the Roads family graveyard out under the cottonwoods by the creek. He dismounted by the two recent graves. Then he spat on Joby's.

"If I wasn't a God-fearing man, Joby Watkins, I'd dig you up and throw you in the canyon. Your bones could bleach there for all I care. But I will do this."

He reached down and pulled out the wooden marker with Joby's name on it. "You don't deserve to be remembered alongside my nephew, Jimmy." He kicked some leaves over the gravesite and spat again. Nettie took his arm.

"You don't have to leave him here with your ma and pa and Jimmy, Garrett. You can move him out to the back of the ranch and forget him. Now come on inside. We'll get a fire going and cook up some of this food we got in town."

Roads nodded. "All right, Nettie, all right."

★★★

Later that night, the three travelers sat in front of the fire, thinking about the long trail they had ridden over the past months. Roads had discovered his pa's Meerschaum pipe on a shelf, along with a stash of tobacco, and he was sitting silently in an old chair, puffing contentedly and watching the coals. Nettie and Budrow sat together on the couch. Finally, Roads spoke.

"Ya'll probably wondering what passed between me and Alice back there. Well ..." he paused for a puff. "She told me what happened here, then she let me know that any man she killed after she left here deserved killing. She's got her gang now, and except for two men left over from The Ten, they are all women. I know there are a couple of Comanche gals, and the rest are probably Texicans uprooted by the war—husbands dead, ranches taken over by carpetbaggers, and the like."

Budrow sipped at a cup of coffee sitting on the small table in front of the couch. "Sounds like a cotillion I'd rather not attend."

"She doesn't want me after her anymore. She's found a new life, and she wants to see where it takes her—with no interference from a self-righteous brother. And as I see it now, I should have known it was Joby all along, and Alice was just being true to herself."

Nettie nodded. "I tried to tell you, Roads."

"I know, Nettie, but sometimes you have to thump me good to get me to see the light."

Budrow smiled. "Glad it's settled, Granite."

"So what now, Kit?"

Budrow looked down at Nettie, who snuggled up close. "Nettie and I have been talking it over, and we have decided to let bygones be bygones."

Nettie grinned. "I figured out something on this last trip. I may be tough, but I'm not a man. Never was, never will be. And as I see it, there's a distinction between me and Kit, both physically and emotionally."

Roads grinned. "I was wonderin' when you would figure that one out. So what are you going to do about it?"

"I asked Nettie to marry me, and she said yes. That's about as brass tacks as I can make it."

"Then what, Budrow? Go back east and live the life you were so accustomed to?"

Budrow shook his head. "Can't. I still have that conviction hanging over my head. I got a letter from my sister about a year ago, and it seems the colonel in charge of my trial is now a bigwig in Washington. I'm afraid my father swallowed his story hook, line, and sinker. Therefore, I am still *persona non grata* back on the old plantation."

"We're gonna look for a little place near here," said Nettie. "Homestead it, raise some cows, you know."

Roads took a draw on his pipe. "I got a better idea."

Budrow perked up. "What ya thinkin'?"

"I need a partner, Kit. I've got a thousand deeded acres here and four thousand more free-range acres I can run cattle on. I can't do it by myself. If I stayed here alone, I'd probably end up spending most of my time in that rocker out front with a bottle of red likker as my only companion. You throw in with me and I'll go shares with you, fifty-fifty."

Budrow stared at his friend. "That's a mighty generous offer, Granite."

"I've been thinking on it for some time. Here's what I know. A man can't go through life by himself, especially out here. This is Texas. It's as big a country as God ever made, and it needs pards who will ride the river together and stand up for each other. Oh, a man can get a wife ..." He lifted his cup to Nettie, who blushed. "... but he needs more than that. He needs real friends." He paused. "Remember when we met, and you said your friends call you Kit, and I said I ain't your friend, Budrow?"

Budrow nodded. "I sure do."

"Well, there's a lot of water under the bridge since then, and that has changed. I'm proud to call you my friend, Kit."

Budrow looked down at the floor, his jaw working. "That's mighty generous of you, pard. But I can't just take half your ranch."

"Didn't you hear me? I need a partner, and I want you. And by all that is holy, you'll earn every acre you live and die on. So just shut up and say yes."

Nettie gave Budrow a swift kick in the ankle.

"Owww, what did you do that for?"

"Take the deal, Kit. You'll never get another like it. And I know a lovely little meadow just down the creek where we can throw up a cabin. We'll make this ranch bigger than Goodnight or Chisum."

Roads grinned. "Listen to your sweetheart, Kit. She'll make a man out of you yet."

Budrow stood up, and so did Roads. Kit put out his hand, and Roads took it. "You got a partner, Granite Roads, and proud to be called your friend too. Now, let's break out that bourbon sitting on the shelf over there and drink to the Roads Ranch."

Granite smiled. "The Roads-Budrow Ranch."

He brought down the bottle, opened it up, poured them each a drink. Then he lifted his glass. "The Roads-Budrow Ranch."

They all lifted and drank.

***

Later that night, Nettie stood alone at the window, gazing out at the Texas night sky.

I wonder where Claret and Annette are tonight.

ABOUT THE AUTHORS

Patrick E. Craig has published books with Harvest House Publishers, Harlequin Books and Elk Lake Publishing as well as his own imprints, P&J Publishing and Islands Publishing. He has written eleven novels including the award-winning Islands series with Murray Pura and two best-selling Amish series, Apple Creek Dreams and The Paradise Chronicles. He lives in Idaho with his wife, Judy.

Murray Pura is a winner of the Hemingway Award, along with co-author Patrick Craig, for the WW2 novel *Far on the Ringing Plains*. He's also won awards for his novels

The Sunflower Season and *The White Birds of Morning.* He works with Elk Lake, HarperCollins, Barbour, and other publishing houses. He lives and writes in the Rocky Mountains of southwestern Alberta.

OTHER ELK LAKE BOOKS
by PATRICK E. CRAIG AND MURRAY PURA

ANTHOLOGIES

The Amish Menorah and other Stories (The Men of Amish Fiction)

A Christmas Collection (The Men of Amish Fiction)

Christmas from the Heart (Elk Lake Authors' Christmas Romances)

PURA & CRAIG

Beyond the Red Hills

The Drive

PURA

Uzura Seki—Black Sands, a Short Story

The Light at St. Silvans

CRAIG

THE ADVENTURES OF PUNKIN AND BOO

The Mystery of Ghost Dancer Ranch

The Lost Coast